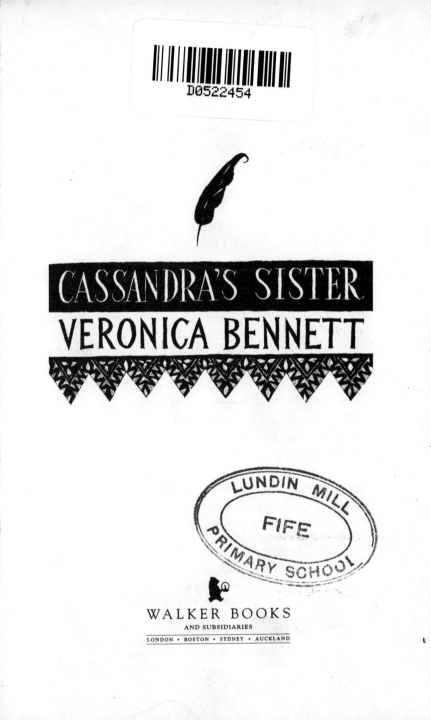

CASSANDRA'S SISTER
VERONICA BENNETT

LUNDIN MILL
FIFE
PRIMARY SCHOOL

WALKER BOOKS
AND SUBSIDIARIES

LONDON · BOSTON · SYDNEY · AUCKLAND

First published 2006 by Walker Books Ltd
87 Vauxhall Walk, London SE11 5HJ

2 4 6 8 10 9 7 5 3 1

Text © 2006 Veronica Bennett
Cover illustration © 2006 Jeff Fisher

This book has been typeset in M Bembo and Stuyvesant ICG

Printed and bound in Great Britain by Creative Print and Design (Wales), Ebbw Vale

British Library Cataloguing in Publication Data:
a catalogue record for this book
is available from the British Library

ISBN-13: 978-1-84428-147-3
ISBN-10: 1-84428-147-7

www.walkerbooks.co.uk

For my sister

PROLOGUE

Paris, 1794

The brightness of the sky smote Jean's eyes so violently that he stumbled. He let out a cry of pain. Then the butt of a guard's rifle landed hard between his shoulder blades, taking his breath away.

In the darkness of the prison cell he had prayed that God would save him. He had reasoned that since God knows everything, He must know that many thousands of innocent men and women had perished beneath the guillotine's blade in the last few months. God surely knew that all Frenchmen, whether sympathetic or hostile to the Revolution, were now calling these months "The Terror". But did God know how much longer the bloodshed would last? Months? Years? Until Jean's beloved France had no more martyrs to make, and no more sacrifices to offer?

Now, thrust into the waiting tumbril, his hands tied behind his back, Jean knew that praying was useless. God had not heard him.

His blood buzzed in his ears, louder and louder, in rhythm with the hammer-beats of his heart. Crouching in the corner, he pressed his head against the cart's wooden rail. He did not want to look at that vast sky, whose brilliance, even on this cold February day, was evidence of the glorious work of the God who had forsaken him.

More and more men were pushed in behind Jean until the tumbril was crammed as full as those he had seen on his estate in the Marais, crowded with animals on their way to slaughter. Trusting beasts, desperate human beings – what did it matter whose blood was shed? Around him, each face told the same story. These men had been condemned for a careless word, or an accident of birth, or because they had tried to protect a loved one.

My Eliza! Swaying in the cart, his heart filling his chest, Jean felt the cold sweat of fear on his face.

Everyone had heard tales of heroism in the face of execution: men who struggled, defying their fate until the end; women who went meekly to their deaths, exposing their white necks to the blade with never a tremble or a cry. But Jean was no hero. He felt neither defiance nor meekness, but true terror. He could not hold up his head before the jeering spectators.

A young man, whose frail body pressed against Jean's, was sobbing. He pawed at Jean's clothes, seeking the comfort of an embrace before he was sent to his grave. But Jean, with his wrists bound, could not give it; neither could he find any words of consolation. This wretch was going to die, but so was Jean, at the age of forty-four. And did this boy have a son, and a beautiful wife to leave behind?

He tried to conjure Eliza as he had last seen her. But his imagination was flooded by the memory of her dark eyes, bright with tears. A cold drizzle had been falling on the day she had taken leave of him after their brief stay in the English city of Bath. His little son Hastings had fretted, reaching out for the carriage which waited to take him and his mother home to London. But Eliza's lovely eyes, tormented by anxiety, had looked into Jean's. "I will return to France, Jean," she had promised. "When this madness is over, I will return." With those words she had kissed him, and stepped into the carriage.

That had been three years ago, in the spring of 1791. The Revolution had been in its infancy. Jean had still felt reasonably safe, far away from Paris at his beloved estate in the Marais. The beginning of the Terror was still years off. They had assumed Eliza would be able to take refuge in England during the conflict, returning to him as soon as it was resolved.

A vain hope. Jean raised his head as the tumbril stopped. There on the platform stood the guillotine, the instrument of his death. A thunderous, merciless noise arose from the crowd, jostling one another and holding children aloft to afford them a better view.

The contraption – what else could one possibly call such a complicated assembly of wood, metal and rope? – rose high, higher than he had imagined. The blade hung at the top. Jean gazed up at it. Angled, sharp, malevolent. Suddenly he knew he was going to vomit. He leaned over and spewed onto the cobbles the remains of the bread he and his fellow-condemned had shared that morning. Bound, he was unable to wipe the bitter taste from his mouth.

The din increased as the prisoners were hauled out of the cart and pushed towards the wooden platform. Blank-faced revolutionary soldiers tried to quell the surge of spectators. Jean saw women younger than Eliza, chanting and stamping with joy at the prospect of witnessing his execution. *Women*, whose God-given nature was to create life, not destroy it! Eliza had been quite right. The Revolution was madness.

Evidently, he was to be dispatched first.

The guards thrust him to his knees before the bascule. Jean trembled as they tied him to it, face-down. He felt his necktie being roughly loosened.

"Thank God," he managed to utter aloud, "that my wife does not know of this moment!"

God had, after all, shown some mercy. Safe in England, with correspondence next to impossible, Eliza had been spared the news of Jean's imprisonment. When news of his death would get to her, and by what means, Jean could not predict. Only one thing was certain: he had no need to fear that she or Hastings would be neglected. Eliza's English relatives would take care of that.

He felt the bascule tip, lowering his body into position. The metal collar secured his bare neck. He closed his eyes, and saw again the pallor of Eliza's face, and the mingling of her tears with the English drizzle.

But there was no time to wish her farewell. The blade completed its travel in less time than it took to say the three syllables of her name.

BOOK ONE

Beheaded

Eliza

As Jenny and her sister neared the Rectory the heat was going from the day. The sunshine crossed the walls of the house at a steep angle, plunging half the garden into shadow. The stock-scented air was perfectly still. Cassandra opened the gate. Full-leaved gooseberry bushes brushed Jenny's skirt as she followed her sister up the narrow path to the kitchen door.

"When do you suppose Henry will return from Basingstoke?" asked Cass.

"Soon, I hope, since it is already two hours past dinner time. But of course it is impossible to start dinner without the greediest person in the family."

"Henry is tall and strong," protested Cass. "He needs to eat large meals."

"Defend him to the last, if you will, though you are quite aware that my approval of our incorrigible brother is bound-less. And anyway, *I* am so hungry I could eat the very horse he is riding home on."

Cassandra laughed. Then, abruptly, she stopped laughing. "Look!"

A carriage stood in the lane where the garden met the fields. Not a light trap such as local people used for calling at the Rectory, but a large, highway-travelling carriage with muddy wheels and dust-covered windows. Although no horse was hitched to it, its arrival was clearly very recent.

"Do you recognize it?" asked Jenny warily.

The war with France had not only taken Henry into the army, but their younger brothers, Frank and Charles, into the navy, and the sisters lived with the ever-present possibility of distressing news. A feeling Jenny recognized only too well, as if she had laced her stays too tightly, began to rise up inside her.

"No," admitted Cass. But to reassure her younger sister she added, "It is probably visitors for Papa. The parents of a prospective pupil."

Jenny knew it was not. Parents of prospective pupils did not come until later in the summer, and never from very far away. This carriage had come a great distance.

"I shall go in first, if you wish," offered Cass.

"No, let us go together."

The open kitchen door revealed the unusual sight of the housemaid standing on a chair.

"Oh, miss!" the girl exclaimed when she saw Cassandra. She began to untie her apron. "Mistress said I was to fetch you to her as soon as you came in."

Cassandra set down the laden basket their sister-in-law had given them. "Never mind about that now, Kitty. Tell me, whose carriage is that in the lane?"

But before the girl could reply Mama entered the kitchen, her best cap, hurriedly put on, covering only half her head. "Girls!" she cried. "Why did you not come to the front door?" She caught sight of the basket. "Oh, preserves! How kind Anne is!" She advanced upon her daughters open-armed. "Come, let me embrace you, my dearest, dearest girls! Such dreadful news!"

This display of affection in the presence of a servant convinced Jenny that there had indeed been a death in the family. "Mama, tell us at once," she urged. "What in the name of God has happened?"

"Eliza's husband is dead!" announced Mama. Reluctantly, she released her daughters. "Eliza is in the drawing-room," she told them, her voice faltering. She put her handkerchief to her eyes. "Oh dear, I know not what to say!"

Jenny could not swallow the lump that constricted her throat. It troubled her greatly to see her mother's distress. Eliza, though Mama's niece only by marriage, enjoyed her aunt's great favour, indulgently bestowed. For her own part, Jenny loved Eliza well, though her affection had always been tempered with awe for her older, worldlier cousin.

Cass picked up her skirts decisively. "Come, let us join them."

The evening sunlight beat so strongly on the windows that the drawing-room resembled a splendidly lit stage. Upon the instant they entered Jenny was transported back to Christmases past, when Eliza had encouraged her young cousins to act plays at the Rectory for themselves and their relatives. Every boy and girl in the house had joined in with such enjoyment that Jenny often regretted that they had all grown up and could no longer behave in such a fearlessly inelegant way.

Eliza was now *very* grown up – over thirty – but as she stood before the window, her mourning dress no less exquisite than any other outfit Jenny had ever see her in, she still held something of the bold theatricality which had enchanted them years ago. The bright light made it clear to Jenny, however, that anxiety and grief had made their mark on her cousin's once resplendent beauty. Eliza was still delightful to look at, but her face looked pale, almost white, against the brim of the black bonnet that recent widowhood demanded. The brown of her eyes, a deep brown like Papa's, remained the same, but the expression they had held in her youth, which Mama used to call "tigerish", had gone. She looked, Jenny realized, diminished.

"My dears!" Eliza took her cousins' hands and kissed their cheeks. Jenny remembered how the same scene had taken place in this very room, two years before, when Eliza's adored mother had died. Then, as now, Eliza had quit London and sought sanctuary in the country vicarage with her mother's brother and his family. *What do we offer her,* wondered Jenny, *which her friends in London cannot?*

There were three other people in the room. Papa stood with his back to the unlit fire, his feet planted some way apart. Asleep in the corner of the sofa lay Eliza's son Hastings, watched over by Madame Bigeon, who acted as Hastings's nurse and Eliza's *bonne*, as elegantly dressed as ever but pale with exhaustion. Her eight-year-old charge, afflicted since birth by a weakness of the brain and great physical delicacy, was not an easy one.

Jenny's heart would not quiet itself. She longed, yet dreaded, to hear the story of what had happened to Jean Capot de Feuillide. Revolution and war, two such vivid players on the stage of history, might seem far away from her quiet family in their rectory in the Hampshire countryside. But they were not.

Mama went to her husband's side. "George, the girls do not yet know the entire story."

"*I* shall tell them, Aunt," Eliza cut in. "I cling to the hope that the more times I say it, the less terrible the word will sound." Releasing Cass and Jenny's hands, she resumed her place by the window. "Guillotined, my dears," she said, giving the terrible word as little consequence as she could. "Three months ago."

"Dear God!" breathed Cass, her eyes filling. She sank into a chair. "May the Lord have mercy upon his soul."

"He went to Paris," explained Eliza. As she spoke, her fingers gently smote the window-frame in a rhythmic accompaniment to her words. "He should never have left the Marais, but he needed money. He had to see his bankers. When he was there he heard of an old friend who had been wrongly imprisoned for conspiring against the Revolutionary government, and tried to help him. Foolish, foolish Jean! Of course he was arrested too. He was tried, found guilty of the same crime as his friend and guillotined within days."

The shafts of light had lengthened as the sunk sank; the room was shady. The sleeping Hastings gurgled and blew, shifted, and was quiet.

"However, I have the comfort of knowing he did not languish in prison for months, as some poor wretches do," continued Eliza. "His end, once set in motion, was swift. I received news of it from the bankers in Paris. They had written several letters, but correspondence from France is so haphazard these days…"

She could not go on. She closed her eyes and bowed her head.

"My dear Eliza!" Papa, his face stricken, went to her side. "This is too distressing for you."

But she shook her head. "No, Uncle, I shall finish the story."

"At least sit down then," requested Papa. He called for Kitty through the open door, then turned back to Eliza. "You have not rested since your long journey, nor taken any refreshment. Would you not be revived by a glass of wine?"

"Very well. Thank you."

Eliza's legs had lost their strength. She sat down quickly on the chair to which Papa had led her. "Here, let me remove your bonnet," said Cass, concerned. "Oh, Kitty, would you bring Miss Eliza some wine?"

Fanning herself, Eliza expressed her gratitude and resumed her account.

"I received all the bank's letters, bundled together, only yesterday, though Jean was … it was in February that he died. You may imagine my feelings as I read them. I summoned Madame Bigeon at once and asked her to make Hastings ready for the journey. My first thought was to come into Hampshire, where I have always been so happy." She paused, and looked tenderly at the sleeping child. "Hastings will be an Englishman now. The chateau at the Marais has already been sold, and Jean's tenants turned out. I have nothing left in France."

"Then it is as well you have plenty in England!" said Mama with feeling. Again Hastings stirred, and Madame Bigeon soothed him.

"You must stay with us as long as you like, my dear," said Papa.

"You are very kind," said Eliza, with a graceful dip of her

head. "I would very much like to. But I fear my affairs in London will not allow me a stay of more than a few days."

Kitty brought the wine. As Jenny took the glass to hand it to her cousin she saw that the maid's eyes were glossed by unshed tears. She squeezed the girl's hand. "Thank you, Kitty," she whispered.

It was hardly astonishing that Kitty should be affected by the news. She had no personal duties to perform for Eliza, but, like everyone else in Steventon, she must have been struck by the story of the fatherless English beauty who had married a French aristocrat. The heroism shown by the husband of "Miss Eliza" in remaining in France during the appalling events of the Revolution had provided the household – and the village – with gossip enough for every inquisitive ear.

When Kitty had gone Papa walked around the room, sighing. Jenny knew he was praying. "I shall make a sermon on Sunday about the ineffable mystery of God," he announced at last. "We must believe He has a reason for taking de Feuillide from us, and derive comfort from that. My dear," he said to Mama, "do the servants know the truth?"

"Only that Monsieur le Comte has died in France."

"Then let us tell them no more for the present. We shall have prayers later." He looked steadily at Eliza. "Trust in God, my dear. I shall be in the study if anyone should want me."

He bowed, and kissed Eliza's hand with the old-world courtesy some people admired, others ridiculed, but Jenny rejoiced at. She fiercely loved her father and all his mannerisms. This blow to his beloved niece, daughter of a no-less-beloved sister, would fall heavily on his heart.

When he had left the room Cassandra went to Eliza, who had begun to drink her wine. "May I bring you something to eat?"

"No," replied Eliza distractedly. "I thank you, Cass, but..." When she leaned forward to put down her glass, something caught her eye. "Oh! A horseman is stopping here. Another visitor?"

Cassandra looked out. "No, it is only Henry."

The click of riding-boots on the hall flagstones was soon heard. A masculine voice, obliterating poor Kitty's attempts to speak, called for Dick to bring a bucket of water for the horse.

"Fine afternoon for a ride, Kitty! That will do, my boots are clean. Look, not a speck on them. Family down? They have waited dinner, I hope."

When Henry saw Eliza through the half-open drawing-room door he snatched off his hat, put it under his arm, opened the door fully and stood before the company. "Cousin Eliza, what a *very pleasant surprise*! To what do we owe—"

"Henry!" interrupted Mama. "Eliza is not here for a social visit."

"Do not scold him, Aunt," said Eliza. "He has yet to hear my news." She was regarding her son. "Might Madame Bigeon take Hastings upstairs? He will wake soon, and must have his bread-and-milk."

"Of course," said Mama. "Jenny, would you ring for Kitty?"

"Mama, may I show Madame upstairs?" asked Jenny, glad of the opportunity to leave the company. She felt dazed. No, that was not quite right. She searched for a word that described her feelings, and it came to her: *thinned*.

Like watered milk. Eliza's story had entered her soul and weakened her resilience, never very great, to the harshness of the world.

Henry, silenced, watched as Madame Bigeon expertly lifted the child. Jenny longed to run to her brother, hang on his arm, see the realization in his eyes as they fell on Eliza in her widow's weeds. But these were the actions of a child no older than the boy in Madame Bigeon's arms. Instead, she spoke again to her mother.

"If you please, ma'am, I shall stay upstairs until dinner-time." Mama nodded reluctantly, and Jenny turned to Eliza. "Cousin, I beg you to excuse me."

"My dear, of course."

Jenny's longing for solitude had never been so strong. She had neither the patience of Cassandra nor the social ease of Eliza. She could not bear to hear the story of the guillotining repeated for Henry, then to pass the time until dinner in murmured condolences and news of mutual acquaintances.

Madame Bigeon was too fatigued to talk. She asked to be brought bread-and-milk for the boy and soup for herself, with a little bread and wine. Then she retired behind her door.

In her own room Jenny, with inexpressible relief, flung down the bonnet which still hung around her neck, peeled off her gloves and unbuttoned the close-fitting jacket she wore over her dress. How she hated these inconveniently fashionable jackets, so hot in summer and too short to offer any warmth in winter. And where was her parasol? Abandoned in the kitchen, probably, to be tripped over by Mrs Travers, the cook, who would blame Kitty for leaving it there. Not for the first time the thought occurred to Jenny that it was little wonder that men scorned – or, worse still, were unaware of – women's true mental abilities, when all they saw and heard of the lives of the female sex was concerned with tight clothes and trivial objects.

She knelt on the tapestry cushion on her side of the window seat. She and Cass had each adopted "my side", as children will, when this little sitting-room had first been presented to them, and they had never broken the habit. Jenny's eyes felt hot. She rested her brow against the cool window pane, which faced away from the sun. The trees at the end of the garden looked black against the twilit sky.

Her heart somersaulted. The trees – tall, still, silent – brought to her mind a vision of that symbol of man's hatred and destruction, the guillotine. She could not make it disappear. Her brain was alive with questions she could neither ask aloud, nor expect to be answered. What had been Jean's thoughts as he mounted the scaffold? Did he have the chance to write a last message to Eliza, or his family in France? Did he break down, or face the blade proudly?

Jenny did not know when she had ever encountered a more distressing thought. She wished she could be calm about it. But the combination of an energetic imagination and a sympathetic nature made her agitated sometimes. And Cousin Eliza, so often the antidote to this woeful tendency, was now its cause. *Jenny, you are making Eliza's bereavement into a drama of your own,* she scolded herself. *Your vanity knows no bounds.*

"God give Eliza strength!" she whispered. "And show me how to act in her presence!"

As the daylight crept away Jenny went on sitting there on the window seat, her head bowed, her hands in her lap, as if she were at church. But she was not praying; neither was she aware of time passing. She was thinking, thinking...

When Kitty came in to inform her that dinner was ready she had not even taken off her boots. "Oh, Miss Jane!" exclaimed the maid anxiously. "Do you not want your slippers? And you still have your jacket on. Let me get your shawl."

Jenny allowed Kitty to help her off with the boots and jacket. "Kitty..." she began.

"Yes, miss?"

"You went to school, did you not, here in the village? You know your letters?"

"Yes, miss."

"Do you ever read novels?"

"Novels, miss?" Kitty, inspecting the soles of Jenny's boots, sounded uncertain.

"Yes. Mrs Radcliffe's, for instance. *The Romance of the Forest*?"

"Oh! Yes, miss, I've looked into that one. Not when I was supposed to be at my work, though, miss, ask Mrs Travers."

"Of course. Those boots are perfectly clean, you know. The lane is quite dry. Do you like romances, or stories which frighten you?"

This time Kitty's bewilderment at being questioned by her young mistress overcame her. She tidied away the boots, folded the jacket, bobbed a curtsey and fled.

Jenny hugged her knees, wondering, wondering... Then she stirred herself, slipped her feet into her soft leather indoor shoes and went to the looking-glass on the wall. A round face regarded her, framed with curls crushed by her discarded bonnet. *You are here, in your room, safely surrounded by those you love*, she told her reflection silently. *But where does Jean Capot de Feuillide lie now?*

Jenny

*J*enny often considered how lucky she was. Unlike the orphaned Eliza, she and Cassandra had both their parents living, and all their brothers too, despite the hazards of the masculine world. Five of these six brothers, including fourteen-year-old Charles, who was at naval college and would take great exception to being overlooked from the list, enjoyed a rudeness of health and brightness of prospect remarked on by many Hampshire friends. James, the eldest, was a clergyman like Papa, and lived close by with his wife and baby girl, while Edward, who was next to Henry in age, had also married and begun his family. Frank, whose place between his sisters made him especially approved of by both, was doing well as a naval lieutenant.

The remaining brother, George, who had a condition similar to that from which Hastings suffered, and had to be cared for away from home, was no less cherished by Mama and Papa than his more robust brothers. For all this Jenny daily thanked God. But a large part of her gratitude was reserved for what she considered an equally great blessing: Steventon itself.

The day after Eliza's arrival she rose early and, leaving Cassandra sleeping, went out into the June morning. She breathed the calm air, surveying the view. However often she saw it, she would not be deflected from the opinion that the landscape of southern England was unequalled in its beauty. Nothing she had seen in art or life could compete with the spring-renewed glory spread before her. Born to it as she was, it never failed to awaken in her a reverence deep enough to be a passion.

The house was only a country rectory, surrounded by a garden which was only a vegetable plot, a few flower-beds, a pigsty and a run for Mama's chickens. Papa's school had room for only a few boys, though, as Mama frequently reminded him, they made up in high spirits what they lacked in numbers. Steventon was only a village like many another, containing the usual mixture of inhabitants, some delightful, some not. But the contentment that this small world gave Jenny was so profound, she could not imagine how she would bear its loss when – if – a young gentleman should ever come to take her away to *his* world.

She wandered up and down the lines of raspberry and gooseberry bushes, holding her skirt away from the ripening fruit. Kitty, in her milking apron, a bucket in each hand, emerged from the dairy and crossed the yard. The sour smell of manure mixed with the sweeter one of the bakehouse. From the kitchen came the sound of Mrs Travers alternately scolding Kitty and singing while she prepared breakfast. Jenny picked a handful of raspberries and leaned against the sun-warmed garden wall. She crushed a berry against the roof of her mouth, aware that each of her senses felt more than usually alert. The world had never seemed more beautiful, and, mindful of yesterday's heart-stabbing news, she had never been more relieved to be in it.

I am simply the luckiest girl alive, she told herself.

"I would so love to see the Lloyds again" were the words with which Eliza addressed her aunt after breakfast. "Dear Martha and Mary! And Mrs Lloyd, of course."

Scarcely a day went by when Jenny and Cass did not walk to nearby Deane Parsonage. Their particular friend was the elder Lloyd sister, Martha, whose simplicity of nature and keen intelligence had recommended her to them from the day the Lloyds had entered the neighbourhood.

"I am sure a visit can be arranged," said Mama, contemplating the cluttered remains on the table. She could not rise until Hastings had finished, and Eliza was still patiently feeding him porridge.

"Let us go today!" suggested Jenny.

"But they do not expect us," objected Cass calmly. "One cannot go calling on people without notice."

"Oh, the Lloyds never mind about that."

"Jenny!" cautioned Mama. "You forget, this will not be the usual sort of visit. We are in mourning, and must adhere to the formalities, as your sister points out."

"As if I could forget that we are in mourning, Mama!" cried Jenny, mortified to be admonished before her cousin. "I merely meant to say," she explained to Eliza, "that there is no need for us to put off visiting them. They are our closest friends."

"Very well, then," said Eliza, "it is settled. I shall write a note for your servant to take over to Deane this morning, and bring Mrs Lloyd's reply. I am persuaded we shall see them this afternoon."

"Am *I* to be included in the party?" Henry asked, looking at Eliza over the newspaper from his seat by the window. His side-lit features, youthfully bony, looked to Jenny quite handsome. For a brother, anyway.

"Would you like to be included?" Eliza asked him.

"Most certainly," returned Henry. "The Lloyds' cook makes excellent scones."

"Then let us all walk to Deane together," said Eliza. "Hastings must have his airing, and the weather is delightful. Shall you come with us, Aunt?"

"No, I must excuse myself," replied Mama. "I shall be helping Travers bake pies today. I daresay you are not aware, Eliza, of the number of pies needed to satisfy our schoolboys' appetites?"

"Oh…" Eliza looked concerned. "Are you able to spare Cass and Jenny, then?"

"My dear, they are more use in eating the pies than baking them. And as for you, Henry," Mama added, "why not take Mrs Lloyd a jar of that apricot preserve Anne sent over yesterday so that you may spread it on your 'excellent' scone?"

Jenny took note of how lively, and how like Cass's, her mother's eyes were. Jenny had once teased her sister, saying that she was as beautiful as "Classical" Cassandra, the heroine of Greek legend, while she, Jenny, was "Plain" Jane. "You judge yourself too harshly," had been Cassandra's reply.

"*I* shall present the preserves to Mrs Lloyd," volunteered Eliza, taking up a napkin to wipe Hastings's mouth, "since I have no gift of my own to take. If she asks how they are made, however, I must disclaim all knowledge."

Hastings was not able to walk as far as Deane. He was

pushed by Madame Bigeon in an invalid chair stuffed with many cushions. Henry walked beside them, carrying a blanket in case Hastings should feel cold, and a basket of provisions in case he should be hungry or thirsty.

Eliza led the way. "How delightful Steventon is!" she declared, linking arms with her cousins and sniffing the air. "I do believe that scent is honeysuckle. Oh, you have no idea how insufferable sooty buildings and hard pavements are when the sun shines on them!"

It was a long time since Jenny and Cass had visited London, but they were familiar with Bath. Jenny remembered how violently she had hated its slippery cobbles and garish, torch-lit rooms. "We have no doubt of the advantages of Hampshire," she said to her cousin, "but do you not remember the last time you were here? It rained every day, and the ford was flooded."

"I *do* remember!" cried Eliza. "Henry and Edward went to Basingstoke to get that book I wanted, and they arrived back as bedraggled as if they had been sea-bathing in their street clothes. I never saw our good-natured Edward look so mortified!"

She turned her attention for a few moments to Madame Bigeon, instructing her briefly in French. Then she resumed her place at the head of the party. "Dear Edward. What news of him?"

"His wife, Elizabeth – you have met her, have you not, Eliza? – reports that their little girl, Fanny, is on her feet, and curious about everything in the house," Cass informed her. "Fanny and her cousin Anna, James and Anne's little girl, are the dearest children in the world, are they not, Jenny? Oh! I mean, except for Hastings, of course."

Eliza suppressed a smile at Cass's confusion. "Anna and Fanny must be very near in age."

"Yes," said Jenny. "Last spring Cass and I suddenly became aunts twice over, within a few weeks."

"And do you see your nieces often?"

"We saw Anna only yesterday, when we called on James and Anne," replied Cass. "And though we do not go often into Kent, we hope to visit Edward and Elizabeth at Godmersham later this summer, and look forward very much to seeing little Fanny then."

"Do we?" asked Jenny amiably "I have not heard about this, though I confess I do not listen to every single word uttered by our parents."

To Jenny's surprise, Cass coloured. "It is merely a suggestion," she said uneasily. "I am not sure…"

Perceptive Eliza rescued her. "So James and Edward are each the father of a daughter!" she exclaimed. "And to think I slept last night in the very chamber they shared as boys. Did you know that their heights are still visible, marked on the door-frame?"

"So are ours," said Cass, "on our door-frame. It is an Austen tradition."

"Nobody ever measured *me*, and I am an only child," Eliza observed. Then she gave her head a little shake, and turned to a new subject. "And now, my dear cousins, may I mention the name of *Fowle*?"

Jenny glanced at her sister. She looked very lovely. Fine skin and curly hair, prerequisites of any beauty, were Cass's naturally. But Eliza's words had immediately brought a softness to her eye and a rosiness to her cheek, and her normally serene countenance had grown animated. "You may, Eliza," she said, "provided we are out of earshot of Henry. He does so love to mock the idea of Tom Fowle's actually marrying me, you know."

"Then his impertinence is greater even than I had realized," said Eliza. "Why, he could not hope for a better match for you. Indeed, I have great hopes for another match, Jenny, between you and the younger Fowle."

"Charles," supplied Jenny, knowing Eliza had forgotten the name of Tom's brother.

"What do you say to the notion?" continued Eliza. "Does he please you as much as his brother pleases Cass? Are we to have a double wedding?"

Jenny tried her best not to allow her feelings to colour either her face or her voice. "We are not, Eliza, so you may put away that 'notion' for good."

In truth, Jenny did like Charles Fowle, but only in the same way that she liked any young man who was kind to her. He and his brother had lived at the Rectory when they were Papa's pupils, and although to her childish eyes they had seemed impossibly mature (they were the same age as Henry and Edward respectively), their willingness to help a little girl learn to play cards and to allow her to join in ball games in the garden had made them a much valued part of Steventon life. Later, Tom's superiority in age had ceased to matter, and when Cass was nineteen he had spoken, and she had accepted. Jenny knew that the expectations of her relatives were attuned to the possibility of a further alliance between the two families, but Charles Fowle was ... only Charles Fowle. Try as she might to please everybody, Jenny could not make him into anything more.

"I refuse to be discouraged!" replied Eliza. "Now, another interesting notion has just occurred to me. When I am able, I shall make a point of having you and Jenny stay with me in Orchard Street. I shall prevail upon Tom and Charles to leave their labours for a few days, and we shall all venture out to a ball together. What do you say?"

Cassandra was too bashful to say anything. So Jenny, who felt that she had never loved her cousin so much, replied for both sisters. "Oh, Eliza, you are so kind!"

Eliza turned to look at Hastings. Jenny saw a shadow of emotion cross her face.

"One thing I have learned over the years," she said, watching her son's pleasure as he trailed his hand along the honeysuckle hedge, "is that life is more precious than anything. While we have it, we must live it to the full."

Taking tea in the Lloyds' garden, Jenny was glad Henry had accompanied them. His presence, even if he did not speak – which could not realistically be hoped for – was a relief from the usual domestic cast thrown over these feminine gatherings.

Evidently Mrs Lloyd agreed. "Why, Mr Henry – or should I say Mr *Austen*, now you are grown into such a tall gentleman – how honoured we are!" she beamed, adding hurriedly, and bowing, "Indeed, we are *twice* honoured by the presence of your dear cousin Madame la Comtesse de Feuillide!"

Martha looked embarrassed. Mary smiled. Mrs Lloyd admired Hastings and offered Eliza condolences on the tragic news imparted in the note the Lloyds had received that morning. Eliza nodded her acceptance of these formalities graciously, setting the bunched black ribbons on her black straw bonnet rustling. Jenny saw Mary and Martha eyeing the bonnet, and the lace on Eliza's sleeves, and the fine Indian silk of her shawl, gloves and parasol. Such gorgeous attire was rarely seen in the country, especially in the middle of the afternoon, and must be committed to memory for the benefit of others.

"Now, Mr Henry, tell me what you are about these days," demanded Mrs Lloyd as Martha handed Henry his tea. "Your mama tells me your progress in the militia has been rapid. Where are you stationed?"

"At Petersfield," Henry informed her. "At present I am visiting Steventon for a few days."

"How lucky to have fallen in with Madame la Comtesse!" cried Mrs Lloyd. Then, remembering, "Although of course one might have wished for different circumstances. But Petersfield is so near, you must ride home often."

Henry bowed. He did not ride home often. Army life among men and horses naturally appealed to him more than rectory life among boys and women. But as he was a general favourite, he seemed to Jenny forever able to redeem himself.

"I avail myself of my parents' hospitality whenever my duties allow me," he assured Mrs Lloyd, "though, alas, that is not so often as I would like."

Mrs Lloyd was satisfied, but Eliza spoke up. "Henry, you are a born diplomat. You should be serving the King in a capacity altogether more exciting than the militia." Opening her fan, she whispered loudly behind it to Martha. "Do you not think Henry would make an excellent court adviser? On foreign affairs, perhaps?"

"A *spy*, do you mean?" asked Martha, putting up her own

fan, ready to share in Eliza's charade.

"I would not mention the word."

"If you will persuade His Majesty to install me at court," returned Henry, "buy me a house in London and another in the country, and provide me with a carriage, horses and a pack of hunting dogs, I might consider such employment. Meanwhile I am happy to be a humble soldier."

"Humble?" said Eliza, lowering her fan. "Never!"

The company laughed, and the subject was changed. Eliza was at pains to put everyone at their ease. She listened with sympathy to Mrs Lloyd's complaints about her servants, complimented Mary and Martha on their new white muslins, accepted two cups of tea and gave Mary's pet dog tidbits from her plate. Each time anyone seemed disposed to speak of her loss, she steered them away from it.

Jenny watched with interest. She greatly admired the composure that Eliza had maintained since the moment in the drawing-room when Papa had stood ready to catch her if she swooned. Jenny felt sure that, if thrown into sudden mourning herself, her own behaviour would compare unfavourably. Mama often advised Jenny to curb her sensibility, though Cassandra, ready as ever to defend her sister, always retorted that without it Jenny would scarcely be Jenny.

The company conversed smoothly – Martha was good at managing these tea parties – but Jenny heard none of their words. An idea had come to her. It was an idea so vivid that it blotted out the garden, the tea table, the muslin dresses, the dog, and replaced them with the scene in her imagination. Eliza … of course, *Eliza*! Eliza with her wealth and her tragedy, her social graces, her kindness and beauty and intelligence, and her connections to the highest society of both

Britain and France. Why had Jenny not seen something so obvious before?

"Jenny!" Martha's voice entered Jenny's reverie. "We are speaking of you, and you are not even aware."

"Speaking of me?" repeated Jenny in surprise.

"Madame la Comtesse was saying how much she thinks you have grown since she last saw you. You are taller than Cass now, are you not?"

"A little, I think." Jenny felt her colour rise. Everyone except Henry, who was playing with the dog, was looking at her.

"And we all admire your graceful bearing, you know," went on Martha.

Jenny was bewildered. "Why ... why did this subject arise?"

"I am guilty, I confess," explained Eliza, smiling. "I happened to observe to Martha how lovely you look in that white bonnet. And Martha replied that she would give anything to have curly hair like yours. So I mentioned the clear colour of your eyes – such a true brown! – and the grace of your figure."

"I have inherited Mama's nose!" protested Jenny.

This caused general laughter, and increased Jenny's embarrassment. But Cass came gently to her rescue. "Your modesty becomes you better than any bonnet, Jenny."

"Yes, indeed," said Mrs Lloyd, nodding energetically. "And now, Miss Cassandra, it is *your* turn to be admired. How many months will pass before we can follow you and Mr Fowle to church? You have been engaged these two years, have you not?"

Cassandra hated such questions. Jenny watched her sister,

aware that under the classical-sculpture exterior beat a heart no less passionate than it was patient. She knew that Cass awaited only the signal from Tom to put the first stitch to her wedding dress.

"You will wait more than months, I fear, ma'am," she told Mrs Lloyd. "Tom is the incumbent of a parish which does not provide him with enough money to put anything by for his future. If he cannot get a better living it will be several years before we can be wed."

"You are very sanguine about it, Cass," observed Martha sympathetically. "I should have run out of patience long before two years had passed."

Cassandra paused before she answered. "I *am* sanguine. People tell me it is my nature, but it does not mean I do not long to be Tom's wife. I do, very much. But it is God's will to keep us apart at present. We are young, and can wait a long time."

Jenny felt proud of her sister. Mrs Lloyd was impatient for a wedding, but Cassandra wanted a *marriage*. It was the prospect of the happiness of that marriage which enabled her to wait at Steventon, sewing her trousseau gradually as funds would allow, passing her days quietly among friends and relatives, and writing letters to Tom by candlelight when she thought Jenny was asleep.

"And when shall we see Tom again?" asked Mary.

Cass hesitated, then decided to speak anyway. "You will not see him at Steventon for a long time, but I believe Mama and Papa have some notion of our meeting at my brother Edward's estate in Kent this summer."

Jenny understood why Cass had hesitated. Serious plans *were* afoot, then, to bring Cass and Tom together at

Godmersham. Did Jenny's exclusion from these discussions signal her exclusion from the party? If so, it would not be for the first time. Three years' difference in age *did* matter sometimes, however often people commented on how inseparable the sisters were. Cass was regarded as a woman – twenty-one, calm and practical, blissfully engaged to an equally level-headed man – while Jenny was still seen as a fledgling woman, half-formed, without her sister's polished manners, and her head always full of questions no one seemed able to answer.

"Well, I agree with my daughter, Miss Cassandra," Mrs Lloyd was saying. "You are very patient for one so young. And now, Mr Henry, may we enquire if there is any young lady you are paying your addresses to? I suppose the fair creatures of Petersfield have been introduced to you and your fellow officers?"

Henry bowed politely, but would not be drawn on the subject. Jenny was not surprised. Henry was attractive to young ladies, certainly, but like Tom Fowle he had no fortune. He could not contemplate marrying until he had made money from the army or some other source. She also knew, better than Mrs Lloyd, that he was sensible of the fact that in time of war, any serving militia officer could be required by the regular army at short notice. He was not prepared to inflict the cruelty of daily anxiety upon those he left behind.

They left the Lloyds late, Hastings and his nurse having gone back to the Rectory after tea. All four were fatigued as they trundled homeward in Mrs Lloyd's trap, pulled by her slow old pony, driven by her slow old coachman.

"How dull our country life must seem to you," said Henry to Eliza ruefully. "And Mrs Lloyd is extremely interested in other people's marriages, is she not?"

"Mrs Lloyd is a dear lady without malice towards anyone," said Eliza. "But her habit is to speak her mind."

"And she has two daughters past marrying age," observed Jenny.

"I flatly refuse to marry either Martha or Mary Lloyd!" cried Henry.

"You see?" said Eliza. "Country life is not dull at all. Engagements and weddings and – what did she call them? – the fair creatures of Petersfield?"

Henry answered with a contemptuous look.

"I know you despise such things, Henry," said Eliza, "but your parents' hospitality is the very best medicine for me at present. Why else do you think I made my way straight here? I could have all the wailing and tearing of hair I might wish for among my London friends, but I crave the peace of Steventon. The harmless inquisitiveness of your neighbours is far preferable to the speculation about *my* situation which is doubtless taking place at this very minute in Mayfair."

Jenny was unable to discern what expression lay on Eliza's face, shadowed as it was by her hat brim and the dusk. She knew Eliza was resilient by nature, and that her long separation from her husband must ease the pain of his passing. She knew her cousin would face her widowhood boldly, and not dwell on horrors like Jenny herself was wont to do. But it was true that Eliza's "situation" was interesting. She was very rich, very beautiful, and quite alone. Moving in high society as she did, her smallest action would excite speculation. Who would blame her for hiding herself in Hampshire for a while, until the London gossips had whispered their last about the unspeakable manner of her husband's death, and the unknowable nature of her future?

Jenny's thoughts returned to the idea which had presented itself so irresistibly in the Lloyds' garden. Tomorrow, she would start to put it into practice. Once her household duties were done and Cassandra was conversing with Eliza downstairs, she would slip up to the sitting-room and begin. And if people asked where she was, Cass could employ the excuse she that and Jenny used whenever one of them preferred to be undisturbed: their humble servant, the Sick Headache.

"Lady *Susan*?" Cassandra looked up from her work. "Is her name not Lady *Catherine*?"

"No, that was another story, a long time ago. This is a new one, about a wealthy woman with her own house in a fashionable part of London, and several suitors."

Henry and Eliza had left that morning in Eliza's carriage for Winchester, where Eliza had business at the bank. The carriage was to take Henry back to his regiment before bringing Eliza home to the Rectory in the evening.

The sisters were content to have no reason to go downstairs. Jenny took her place at the writing desk, while Cass sat on her own side of the window seat, sewing a velvet cap for Tom to wear while he wrote his sermons in his draughty rooms.

"I am persuaded that Eliza has some hand in the creation of Lady Susan," said Cass, holding her needle up to the light and re-threading it. "Do not deny it."

Jenny was sharpening a pen. "I cannot help it," she admitted. "Eliza's life has always been more like that of a fictional heroine than a real person. Few real people have the Governor General of India for their godfather, do they?"

"True," agreed Cassandra.

"And few Governors General, real or otherwise, have settled quite so much on their goddaughter," continued Jenny. "Henry says she has five thousand pounds a year. Do you think that is true?"

"It is not my habit to believe anything our brother says until it can be proved," said Cassandra, smiling. "And you should not repeat gossip, you know."

"Even to you?"

"Well…"

"To be serious, Cass," said Jenny. "As if Eliza's situation in life were not unusual enough, are you not also struck by her conduct? She remains calm, and kind, and as delightful company as ever."

"She bears her misfortunes nobly," said Cassandra, taking up her work again.

"She is truly inspirational. But I am not thinking of writing her biography, you know. Lady Susan is a fictional character whose experiences may have *something* of Eliza's in them."

"Of course," said Cass reasonably.

"I beg you, Cass, do not speak of this to her, or anyone."

"Speak of what, dearest?"

Jenny dipped the pen in the ink and returned to her writing. She could make Lady Susan do whatever she chose. She was not going to look like Eliza; she would make her fair-haired, with flashing sapphire eyes. And she was going to be wicked, which Eliza most decidedly was not. What was the point of a heroine who was good? Heroines, in Jenny's estimation, had to be beautiful, unscrupulous, rich and unencumbered by parents. Heroes, meanwhile, were handsome, *very* rich and almost, but not quite, a match for their lady's quick wit.

Jenny chewed the end of the pen, a habit condemned by Mama as unacceptable even in the least hygienic of schoolboys. She thought hard. Of course, women like Lady Susan were not to be emulated: women must remain truly, not merely *apparently* good, or the world would end in chaos. Everyone knew that. But without writing an actually *immoral* story – imagine what Papa would say if she did! – Jenny longed to produce something which examined the *world*. Each day that passed convinced her that if a woman was rich enough, she could appear to be ruled by modesty and inferiority on the outside, while privately doing exactly as she pleased.

Late that evening Jenny left Cassandra by the drawing-room fire reading Fordyce's Sermons with Papa, and retired to bed. Her exertions in the adventurous society of Lady Susan had exhausted her. But soon after she had snuffed out her reading candle she heard carriage wheels, and footsteps on the stairs. Then someone gently opened her bedroom door. "Are you awake?"

Jenny opened her eyes to see her cousin, still in her outdoor clothes. The candle she carried spread a flickering halo under her bonnet brim.

"Why, Eliza!" Jenny sat up. "Yes, I am perfectly awake. What is the matter?"

"Nothing of importance." Sitting on the edge of the bed, Eliza set the candle down. "I merely wanted to talk. I do not wish to go to bed, though I told them downstairs that I did. Will you humour my mood and listen to my nonsense?"

"I am glad to," said Jenny, thrilled that Eliza had elected to speak to *her*.

Eliza's tone of resignation was clear. "I must return to London tomorrow. Pressing affairs in town take me away, and who can say when they will free me to return again?"

"Is it the bank?" guessed Jenny.

"It *is* the bank, you clever thing." Eliza picked up the candle and held it between her face and Jenny's, illuminating both. There was surprise, but indulgent surprise, in Eliza's eyes. "Why, I daresay you know more of my business than I do myself!"

"I watch people," confessed Jenny. "I look at the expressions on their faces, and I listen to their voices. When you said 'pressing affairs' I knew you were really saying 'money'."

"Oh, how right you are!" sighed Eliza. "Money rules us all. It turns perfectly reasonable people into criminals, and misers, and sinners."

"Yet if we do not possess it, we are equally ruled by its absence," observed Jenny.

Eliza contemplated her in the candlelight. "Are you disappointed that your father can give you no fortune?"

"I have long ago resigned myself to it."

"Cass may be prepared to wait for Tom, but when you fall in love, will you be as patient, my little Jenny?"

"I doubt it," said Jenny solemnly. Then she added, more brightly, "But who is to say I *shall* fall in love? No one in the least eligible ever seems to cross my path."

"That is not true," Eliza asserted. "Why, at the Lloyds' yesterday I heard three or four young men mentioned. Who is Mr Blackall? And Mr Portal? Are they not eligible?"

"Samuel Blackall!" Jenny was scornful. "The older ladies of this neighbourhood have long suspected me of an attachment to Mr Blackall, who has been in and out of the district these five years, and always calls on all the young ladies. But, Eliza, I do not have an attachment to him, nor ever will have. And John Portal is not interested in girls like me. He has higher standards."

"Oh, Jenny," sighed Eliza, "you are prettier than you know. You will soon attract suitors without having to exert yourself at all."

"Will they be suitors I like, though?"

"I am confident of it. If Mr Blackall and Mr Portal will not do, you may be sure that another Samuel or another John, or an Edward or a Robert will."

Jenny began to speak, then hesitated.

"What is it?" asked Eliza. "What were you about to say?"

"I was merely going to observe that even if suitors *do* make addresses, not every woman *can* be married. Fate deals differently with different people. And I sometimes think that if a woman is accomplished, and intelligent, will marriage sufficiently employ her talents?"

"But if you were an accomplished, intelligent *man*," said Eliza, smiling, "do you not think you would like to marry a woman who could match you?"

"Of course," Jenny acknowledged, "and I have my own parents' happiness as daily proof of that. But I cannot help noticing that if a woman without fortune does not marry, her only alternative is to rely for the rest of her life upon family or charity."

Eliza pondered. "Not quite. She could be a governess. Many accomplished and intelligent women are, to be sure."

"But is that not because it is the only employment open to them?" returned Jenny.

She could not contradict her cousin's well-meaning

suggestion. But a governess! Could there be worse torture than living in a house not your own, teaching children whose treatment of you reflected their parents' low estimation of your worth? Rather be married to whoever would take you, and teach your own children, than be a slave to others' whims.

"No, it is not the only employment open to them," continued Eliza. "Respectable women can become writers, whether they are married or not. Consider Miss Burney, the author of *Evelina*, a novel universally admired. And do not pretend the notion has never occurred to you that *you* might earn your living by your pen some day, Miss Jenny. You are always scribbling stories."

Jenny did not ask aloud the questions she so often found herself asking in private. For all women's *story*-writing, where were the female philosophers, physicians, dramatists, scientists? Where were the women's public schools and universities where they could become scholars? Until such institutions existed, women had little choice but to accept their time-honoured lot. And at eighteen years old, with the irrefutable knowledge that she could equal any of her brothers in reasoning, was it truly a comfort to Jenny to be told she was not as plain as she thought she was?

"You see, my dear Jenny," Eliza was saying, "happiness in life comes from many sources. Earning one's own bread may be a great accomplishment, but so is the bearing and raising of children. And the lifelong companionship of a beloved spouse is surely the most profound good fortune any of us can hope for."

"Indeed," agreed Jenny, mindful that Eliza must be thinking of her own cruelly-shortened marriage. "But how many women must marry a man they do *not* love, to secure financial protection and have the children they desire? *That* is my objection to the way of the world. I cannot imagine how unhappy such a situation must be, and yet it takes place every day. If a man *I* did not love…"

She stopped, feeling the blood come into her cheeks. Eliza swiftly took her hand.

"For many women, rather older than you are, it is a better choice than remaining single. And when there are few available men, they must shift for themselves. Why, even my dear late mama was obliged to travel all the way to India to find a husband. And of course she *did* meet my father, and my most excellent godfather."

Eliza stroked Jenny's hand while she talked. In the candlelight the pallor of her face showed yellow; the shadow of her lashes lay upon her cheeks. "When I was young," she went on, "I felt like you do. I hated – *hated* – the notion that a woman's life, body and soul, can be exchanged for money. I considered it another form of Indian trade, as much as that in silks or spices."

Jenny's heart filled with compassion for the brave husband-seeker of forty years ago, and for the young Eliza, appalled that her mother had been driven to embark on such a journey. "Oh, Eliza!" she exclaimed with true sympathy.

"Yet when I was only one year older than you are now, I was myself married." Eliza released Jenny's hand and drew her hand over her eyes. Her voice was not far above a whisper. "I had money of my own, and I used it to attract the kind of gentleman I sought. I realized what you too have understood, that women are dependent upon marriage for social status, which we cannot achieve for ourselves."

Jenny pictured Eliza's introduction to her French aristocrat. Even in their first glance at each other, beneath the undoubted attraction there must also have been the understanding that a bargain was being made. His title was to be bestowed only on a woman who could bring him a fortune, and her fortune was to be bestowed only on a man who could give her a title.

"Dear Eliza," she said softly, " I am greatly indebted to you for these confidences. I shall remember your words for ever."

Eliza lifted her eyelids, and Jenny saw that her eyes were full of tears. "Money conquers love, Jenny," she said. "It is never the other way around."

Elizabeth

*A*fter the departure of Henry and Eliza, life at the Rectory settled back into its routine. The only man in the house apart from Papa was Dick, who had served the family as manservant, ostler, coachman and gardener since before Jenny was born. The schoolboys had not yet returned from the long summer vacation. Papa fulfilled his church duties and worked in his study, emerging only in the afternoon, his whiskers brushed, to preside over the three o'clock dinner table. And even if Dick had had time to talk, he would not have said anything. He was the most taciturn man Jenny had ever met.

"Do you not feel the want of male company when all our brothers are from home?" she asked Cass. "At Deane Parsonage there are only Martha and Mary, and at Manydown House there are *three* girls."

"Three girls and their brother," corrected Cass.

"Harris Bigg?" retorted Jenny. "Why, he is only thirteen. Cannot you provide me with any grown-up men?"

"Sadly, no," confessed Cassandra. "The only family in this

district with more brothers than sisters is our own. But I believe you know that already."

They had just arrived home from a morning spent with the Lloyds. It was a blustery September day, with restless clouds and an air of impending showers. Cassandra had been quiet during their visit. Jenny suspected she was thinking of Tom, whom she was to meet again in a few days' time at their brother Edward's house in Kent.

"Make haste, girls!" Mama came out of the dining room. "Company is expected within the hour, you know."

"Who is coming?" asked Jenny.

Mama looked from one to the other of her daughters, exasperated by their blank looks. "I told you only yesterday that the Biggs are taking a late dinner with us."

"No, you did—"

"We must have forgotten, Mama," soothed Cass, suppressing her sister. "Are all the Biggs coming?"

"No, we expect Mr and Mrs Bigg and Elizabeth. Now, hurry yourselves!"

"You were lamenting a shortage of gentlemen, Jenny," whispered Cass as they started up the stairs, "but this evening we are to have the pleasure of Mr Bigg's company."

"And of his dull wit and sharp appetite," whispered Jenny. Then, louder, to her mother, "But you know, Mama, it does not signify what we do to improve our appearance, for Elizabeth Bigg is far prettier than the two of us put together."

Mama, halfway to the kitchen, gave Jenny an impatient look. "That may be so, but at least tidy your hair, child. And the skirt of your white gown has not seen a brush these half-dozen outings. Do not bother Kitty, she has enough to do."

"I shall see to Jenny's skirt, ma'am," offered Cass. "Your daughters' beauty may be surpassed by Elizabeth Bigg's, but you need have no fear that the cleanliness of their dresses will be."

In the bedroom Jenny pinned up her hair anew, while Cass tried her best to remove several days' dust from the hem of her sister's best muslin.

"Such a fuss, and it is only the Biggs," complained Jenny. "Mama does not need to impress a family who have been here a thousand times before, and are the most amiable and easily satisfied of guests anyway. The dining table is spread as extravagantly as if the King himself were visiting."

"We must forgive our mother," said Cass. "She loves acting as hostess, and when Eliza arrived so unexpectedly, there was no chance to preside over the preparations such a visit normally demands." A thought struck her, and she gazed at Jenny with widened eyes. "Do you think the other Elizabeth, Edward's Elizabeth, is fussing as much over my visit to Godmersham?"

"Edward's Elizabeth!" echoed Jenny with affectionate contempt. "She has so many servants she will scarcely notice any disruption you and Tom make to her household."

"I must confess," said Cass, spreading Jenny's gown on the bed, "I would rather that were the case than to be fêted like royalty."

"Elizabeth Bigg will wear any attentions Mama cares to give her as becomingly as she wears everything else," said Jenny. "And confess it, Cass, she is such an amiable friend you would rather be in her company than anyone else's."

Smiling, Cass began to unpin her own hair. "*Almost* any-one else's, Jenny."

Jenny returned the smile. "Oh, very well. One Tom Fowle is equal to a hundred Elizabeth Biggs, however delightful every one of them would be."

Cass did not reply. She dipped her head; her face was hidden by her loosened hair. When she did speak it was on a different subject. "How is *Lady Susan* progressing?"

"Oh, I have abandoned her."

"No! Why?"

Jenny pondered, looking at her reflection in the glass. Her hair looked particularly well today, she thought. Deep brown, with a high sheen like the horse chestnuts Papa's boys gathered in the autumn. In Jenny's opinion Elizabeth Bigg's famous blonde curls were no more beautiful than her own brown ones. Or Cass's, for that matter.

"I decided the story was too frivolous," she told her sister. "I am thinking of writing something much truer to life. A reflection of ourselves." She bent nearer the mirror, arranging wisps at her temples. "A perfect reflection of ourselves."

"Have you begun it?" asked Cassandra. "What is its title?"

"So many questions!"

"But you always tell me what you are writing."

"I shall tell you when I have something to tell," said Jenny. She smoothed her skirt. It did look better. "Thank you for doing this, Cass," she said. "Now, are you ready? Let us go down and join Mama, or she will complain that waiting for us is bad for her nerves."

"Jenny, have a care," admonished Cassandra. "She does suffer with her nerves."

"Yes, when she remembers to."

* * *

Elizabeth Bigg was handed from her carriage by her corpulent father, followed by the bright-eyed Mrs Bigg, a woman whose elegance of figure belied the number of children she had borne. As ever when Jenny saw Elizabeth after a short separation, she detected in her countenance something of her cousin Eliza's looks. The same small mouth and large eyes; the same confident air. Slim and girlish, with light colouring, Elizabeth Bigg was neither so exotic nor so elegant as Eliza. But she possessed an air of sweet artlessness which Eliza could never, with all her skill, have achieved.

"Why, Jenny, who dressed your hair?" were Elizabeth's first words. "May I borrow her? Or has she returned to her post in the Queen's bedchamber already?"

Elizabeth's company was always pleasant. She and her younger sisters, Catherine and Alethea, were all in their twenties, all attractive, and near enough neighbours of the Austens and Lloyds for all seven girls to regard one another as solid friends. The Biggs' house, Manydown, was a carriage ride away, but Cass and Jenny had paid them enough visits – the Biggs were great givers of balls – to have long abandoned any need to stand on ceremony in their presence.

Jenny embraced Elizabeth with real affection, skewing the fashionably high crown of her friend's bonnet. "You know I dress my own hair, Elizabeth, so do not tease me."

"How can I stop myself?" asked Elizabeth "Teasing my dearest friends is my favourite pastime."

Mama greeted her guests with handshakes and curtseys. "The Reverend is gone to Winchester on church business, but he will return before dinner," she explained as Kitty took their cloaks. "He will be delighted to see you all."

"And to speak to Mr Bigg about the war, I have no doubt," suggested Mrs Bigg.

"Oh, the war!" cried Mama, opening the door to an immaculately cleaned and tidied drawing-room. "The old men discuss it while the young men do it. I always say the same applies to women, though the subject is marriage!"

"My dear Mrs Austen," said Mrs Bigg in admiration, "you really should write some of your clever thoughts down."

"Oh, *I* am not the writer in this family," replied Mama, "though I do occasionally like to try my hand (an awkward hand, I confess) at poetry. It is my eldest son, James, who most likes to compose, and Jenny has written little entertainments for the family too. Come in, come in, and sit down. Kitty, bring the tray."

Elizabeth took Jenny's arm as they followed their elders. "Little entertainments for the family," she murmured. "I hazard that you would not wish your literary efforts to be so described!"

"It is my punishment for having lived a mere eighteen years, I fear."

"How are you, Elizabeth?" asked Cass warmly. "We have not seen you these three months."

"Perfectly well. But I cannot say the same for this poor bonnet, which I must take off before it is crushed flat. There!"

Installed in a comfortable chair, with the new hairstyle revealed by the bonnet's removal duly admired, Elizabeth resumed. "I have been travelling. And what pleasures it has afforded me! You must try it, my dear Cass. And Jenny, too. How splendid it would be to go about the country together!"

Both sisters laughed, loud enough to incur a frown from Mama, who was ever hopeful of elegant visits rich in intellectual and artistic stimulation. "I am happy that you are enjoying yourselves, my dears," she said archly.

Elizabeth knew her friends' mama well. She bowed her graceful head. "I was recommending your daughters try travelling, ma'am. They find the notion extremely comic, though I consider it an excellent way of educating the female mind."

"Travelling?" repeated Mama, surprised "I am a great traveller, to be sure, at least I was in my youth. But do you mean travelling abroad, Miss Elizabeth?"

Mrs Bigg entered the conversation, her hand reassuringly placed upon Mama's arm. "No, no, my dear. Elizabeth has been to Plymouth this summer, and to the very tip of Cornwall, a place called Land's End. She was struck by its wildness and beauty."

"Indeed I was," Elizabeth informed Mama. "There is no need to travel to the Swiss mountains, when we have such cliffs and crags here in England. And Plymouth was full of enchanting people, all bent on a summer of gaiety. If I attended one ball, I must have attended twenty."

"Twenty balls!" exclaimed Cassandra. "Was anyone of our acquaintance there?"

Elizabeth paused, suddenly self-conscious. She looked at her hands, which lay in her lap, remembered that she carried a fan, opened it and began to fan herself. "Mr Harwood was there, for some of the time."

"Mr John Harwood?" asked Cass.

"The very same."

"Such near neighbours, at Deane House," said her mother, with a significant look at Mama, "and yet Elizabeth seems to have seen more of Mr Harwood in Plymouth than we did in the whole of last year."

"It is not what you think," protested Elizabeth, her voice weary but her eyes bright.

Mama, though doubtless interested to hear more of Elizabeth's Plymouth adventure, could not neglect her duties as hostess. She rose to dispense wine and sweetmeats. Cassandra took advantage of this diversion to say, matter-of-factly, "Speaking of travelling, I am soon to make a visit to my brother Edward's house, Godmersham Park."

"Are you going there alone, Miss Cassandra?" asked Mr Bigg, whose part in such a feminine conversation had hitherto been negligible. Daughters travelling alone, however, was a subject on which he felt qualified to speak. "My Elizabeth did not go to Plymouth alone."

"Although I am over twenty-one, and perfectly capable of conducting myself in public unchaperoned," cut in Elizabeth.

"But you are unmarried, my dear," her mother reminded her gently.

Elizabeth's fan went up another inch. She did not reply.

"She was accompanied by her aunt," her father informed Mama. "A woman of very good sense."

"She had her personal maid too, of course," added Mrs Bigg. "With eleven dresses and jackets, and six bonnets packed, and all the shawls and shoes and things a young lady needs, as well as a heavy jewel-box, the services of a footman would not have gone amiss either, but we were unable to spare one."

Jenny felt their neighbour's want of taste, and could look at neither Elizabeth nor Cass. How long would it be before she was able to pass over such moments with the ease of her sister?

"Cassandra shall not be travelling alone either, Mr Bigg," Mama assured him. "She is to be accompanied to Kent by her eldest brother, James, who will spend a few days on business in London."

"I see," said Mr Bigg. Satisfied that propriety had not been compromised, he settled to the dish of sugared fruits at his elbow.

Elizabeth might have a heavy jewel-box and a lady's maid, but Mama's elder daughter was engaged to be married. Jenny knew it was unrealistic to suppose that her mother would miss this chance to remind Mrs Bigg of her own daughters' deficiency in this respect. She waited for Mama's voice to recount to Mr Bigg the remaining arrangements, and sure enough, it came.

"While in London, James is to meet Mr Tom Fowle, to whom Cassandra is engaged, and bring him back to Godmersham."

Elizabeth was delighted. "A tryst! How romantic! Whose scheme was this?"

Her fan back in her lap, her wine glass at her lips, she looked pointedly at Jenny. "Did it come from the imagination of our own storyteller?"

"Actually, it did not," said Jenny.

"It was nothing to do with Jenny at all," Mama assured Elizabeth. "The family in Kent has long expected a visit from Cassandra, and Tom has some business in London later this month. When my husband heard about this, he immediately suggested that Tom be invited to Godmersham too. Tom is Edward's particular friend, you know."

"Am I to understand, then," said Elizabeth, mock-seriously, "that the schemer of the family is the Reverend? Dear me, we cannot have him invading the province of ladies!"

"Indeed we cannot," laughed Cass. "Though I am grateful for his intervention, and for my brother Edward's hospitality."

"Shall they give a ball, do you think, while you are there?" asked Elizabeth eagerly.

"A ball has been discussed, Miss Elizabeth," Mama told her. "And if one *is* held," she added, turning to Cass, "you may be sure that you and Tom will be asked to lead the opening dance."

The thought of this responsibility silenced Cass, but Jenny seized an opportunity she had long awaited. "Elizabeth, are you and your sisters planning to attend the ball tomorrow, at the Basingstoke Assembly Rooms?"

Elizabeth looked expectantly at her mama. "What do you say, ma'am?"

"I do not see why not," replied Mrs Bigg, sending a glance in Mr Bigg's direction. "If my husband does not object."

"I have never objected to your, or the girls' pursuit of enjoyment," he returned swiftly. "Indeed, I know not why you exert yourself to ask the question. My daughters must be the most tireless dancers that ever lived."

"May Cass and I go, Mama?" asked Jenny.

Mama hesitated. She did not mind the girls going to balls; what she found more problematical was the convention that unmarried girls be chaperoned, this task usually falling to their mother. She considered her nervous disposition adversely affected by public balls, though she would occasionally appear, resplendently attired, at a private one.

Jenny saw by the quick movement of her eyes that Mrs Bigg, without waiting for Mama's agreement, had begun to make plans. "Do not be concerned about a chaperone, Mrs Austen," she said. "I can perform that duty for all the girls. Might your daughters be delivered to Manydown, so that I can take them on from there?"

"Oh, thank you!" cried Jenny before her mother could speak. "Is that not a kind offer, Mama?"

"Very kind," agreed Mama. She, too, was making plans. "What a pity none of my boys are at home. Henry, in particular, always enjoys a ball. But Mr Lyford, the doctor's son usually turns out, I understand." She got to her feet. Carefully, she adjusted the lace on her sleeves. "And I have no doubt whatsoever," she added, "that the family from Deane House will be there, including Mr John Harwood. Now, I believe I hear a horse. My husband is come home, so shall we go in to dinner?"

William

The Assembly Rooms at Basingstoke were not as grand as their name suggested. The hall was not wide enough for its height, and tended to become very hot, as the windows were narrow. But the young people of the district tolerated these inconveniences with serenity, because public balls were the only means of meeting anyone of the opposite sex who was not either in or known to their own family.

Jenny loved dancing. She loved to hear the music, loud in such a confined space. She loved the *tramp, tramp* of shoes on the wooden floor and the *swish, swish* of gowns as the ladies turned at the end of the set. She loved the dusty smell of seldom-worn finery. And when enough punch had been drunk to loosen reserve, she loved the look of shiny expectation on the faces of her partners, who led her to the set with damp hands.

Cassandra threw herself into the preparation. She sewed new ribbons on Jenny's best dress, and mended the hole in the satin slipper which her sister had neglected after her last Assembly Rooms ball. She starched lace and pressed and

perfumed gowns, and made Jenny a headdress of blue ribbons to match her new trimming. With the Bigg girls and
their mother to encourage their high spirits, the girls
mounted the steps to the Rooms in a state of expectation
greater than the occasion afforded.

It was always the same. The anticipation, Jenny remembered as soon as she entered the hall, was ever more
enjoyable than the event. The first part of the evening would
have to be passed in talking with acquaintances on inconse-
quential subjects. She would be obliged to admire everyone's
attire, however bizarre, and accept compliments upon her
own. She must remember whose mother had died, whose
father was ailing, whose daughter was near her confinement,
whose grandchild had recovered from fever, thank the Lord.

During pauses, when the necessity to speak did not present itself, she would be able to survey the collection of
potential dancing partners, from someone's sixteen-year-old
brother to the man who kept the draper's shop in
Basingstoke High Street, and had done so these forty years.
She would not sit down often, because the gentlemen knew
she never forgot the steps or tripped over her gown. But it
would not be until much later, amid red faces and increasing
noise, that she would truly begin to enjoy herself.

"So the Misses Austen are gracing the Rooms tonight, I
see?"

Jenny recognized the voice before she set eyes on its
owner. "Good evening, Madam Lefroy," she said, turning.

"Madam" Lefroy was as English as everyone else but had
married a man with French ancestors, and liked to use the
English version of the French form of address. She raised her
eyebrows. "Why, how delightful to see you girls here! Your

mama did not inform me you would be attending, but let that pass."

Jenny and Cass curtseyed. "It is charming to see you, Madam Lefroy," said Cassandra. "And Benjamin."

Benjamin Lefroy, fifteen years old, with a face as round as his father's and a disposition as merry as his mother's, exchanged a sympathetic smile with Jenny. Each knew the other, and the other's mother, well. He bowed neatly, clicking his heels, and excused himself.

"How tall he has grown!" observed Cassandra, looking after him. "I believe he is taller than our brother Charles, who is two years older."

"Do not say that before Mama," warned Jenny. "Oh, look, here come Mary and Martha." She waved her fan. "Good evening, Mrs Lloyd! Martha, what wonderful feathers!"

"Do you like them?" Greetings were exchanged, and Martha showed off the feathered headdress, sent by a relative to Mary, who had shrunk from wearing it. "Mary is so much more modest than her elder sister, you see," said Martha amiably. "Where is your mama? Did she agree to your coming tonight without her?"

"We came with the Biggs," explained Jenny.

"All of them?" asked Martha. "It must have been a crush in the carriage."

"It was, but we were all so merry, it mattered not at all. And Mr Bigg was not there, of course."

"Of course," repeated Martha, almost laughing. "Or else you would have needed two carriages!"

"Sshh!" warned Jenny, "Alethea and Catherine are behind you."

Martha turned. "They are speaking with two girls I have

never seen before." She turned back to the little gathering. "Let us hope some gentlemen arrive soon, or I fear we shall be dancing with each other." She leaned closer and spoke lower. "I see that Elizabeth Bigg and her mother have engaged the attentions of Mr John Lyford. Well, they are welcome. If he asks *me* to dance I shall refuse."

"You will not," predicted Jenny. "It is very difficult to refuse a gentleman when he is standing before you. The trick is to avoid being asked in the first place."

"True. But Elizabeth Bigg has not avoided it. See, she is curtseying to him. How lovely she looks this evening! Perhaps if we stay away from her, if that is possible in a room this size, we shall get some offers from people's fathers and uncles."

"To be sure. Though we can always dance with Ben Lefroy. He is at least tall, as Cass pointed out to his doting mama."

"Did she?" Martha laughed softly. "Dear Cass. If only her Tom were here, or his brother Charles, whom I have always considered personable."

All this was exchanged as Jenny and Martha threaded their way between knots of nervous girls, fanning themselves and breaking into unprovoked giggles. Martha nodded her feathers and Jenny her ribbons to their many acquaintances as they passed.

Alethea Bigg caught sight of them. "*What* a lack of gentlemen!" she cried. "We should have brought Harris!"

All three girls laughed. "By the time Harris achieves eligible status," said Martha, "I shall be even more of an old maid than I am already, and Jenny will be a famous author. No, there is nothing for it but to wait by the wall for whatever comes our way."

"Or rely on Madam Lefroy," suggested Alethea. "She never gives up trying to match-make me and my sisters with her nephews. I daresay she would do the same for you if you prevailed upon her."

"I do not want a Lefroy nephew," said Jenny, mock-peevishly. "I want a dashing stranger, with a fortune and a magnificent seat in the most beautiful county in England."

The other two smiled indulgently. "You are asking a great deal, Jenny," said Martha. "Your disadvantage is that most of the single men in the vicinity happen to be your brothers!"

They laughed again. Jenny started to enjoy herself. It was very pleasing to stand among such warm-hearted friends, criticizing or admiring familiar back-views, feeling perfectly at ease. Her "disadvantage", as Martha had called it, was not so great.

"Jenny!" Cass emerged from the crowd. "I have had an offer for the first dance from Madam Lefroy's brother-in-law," she announced breathlessly. "Apparently, he arrived at Ashe this evening unexpectedly, and when Reverend Lefroy told him Madam and Ben were gone to the Rooms, he decided to join them. Are you not impressed at my conquest? Although he has asked Mary, too."

"Is this not marvellous?" asked Martha dryly. "If you had been there, Jenny, he might have asked you as well."

"But, Martha, he is by no means an unacceptable partner," protested Cass solemnly. "He may be over fifty and as grey-haired as Papa, but he is charming."

"He would be even more charming if he had a son, perhaps?" suggested Alethea.

"Oh no, a Lefroy nephew!" groaned Martha.

"He does have a son, actually," said Cass, "though he is

not here this evening. The family lives in Ireland, I understand. This Mr Lefroy came over to London for a friend's wedding, and decided to call on his brother, Reverend Lefroy, quite at the last minute. Madam Lefroy has only met him once before, at her own wedding."

"So the son remains a mere rumour," concluded Martha. "Still, the father is better than nothing, if, as you say, Cass, he has the charm of the Irish."

The first dance began. Jenny saw Cass with a thin, upright man in an old-fashioned, frogged tailcoat. Elizabeth Bigg had indeed failed to avoid dancing with John Lyford. Watching him lead Elizabeth's fashionably dressed figure down the dance, Jenny wondered why he came repeatedly to balls, parties and dinners without succeeding in attaching anyone. John Lyford was destined to follow his father into the medical profession and was therefore an eligible prospect as a husband, and he was by no means the plainest man she had ever seen. What was it about him that so repelled people – even Martha, that most generous of souls?

"Do you not consider Mr Lyford's eyes to be too close together?" asked Catherine Bigg, who had joined Jenny at the side of the room.

"Yes," agreed Jenny. "But a man can have worse faults."

"Why, Jenny!" exclaimed Catherine. "Are you prepared to dance with him?"

"If he asks me. I never did learn how to refuse."

"Have a care. He is famously boring, you know."

"Have you ever spoken to him?"

"No, but Alethea has, and Mama says—"

Jenny did not hear Catherine's mama's pronoucement upon Mr Lyford. Her hand, and her attention, were seized by Madam Lefroy.

"Are you not dancing, Miss Jenny? And you, Miss Catherine? I can soon remedy that."

Two gentlemen stood behind Madam Lefroy. Jenny recognized one as John Portal, the son of a local landowner, who sometimes went hunting with Henry. The other, the younger, was a stranger.

"This is Mr William Heathcote," beamed Madam Lefroy. "Mr Heathcote, let me present Miss Jane Austen and Miss Catherine Bigg."

Mr Heathcote was the most beautiful man Jenny had ever seen. Acutely aware that Catherine must be equally impressed by his handsome face, she curtseyed as elegantly as she could, and lower than usual. "We are honoured, sir," she said before Catherine could speak.

"And Mr Portal you know, of course."

John Portal, blessed by good looks and an easy manner himself, bowed neatly to the girls. "Delighted, ladies."

Madam Lefroy was beside herself. "Is this not a wonderful surprise? First of all my brother-in-law arrives at Ashe and insists upon joining us here, then our dear friend Mr Portal appears with Mr Heathcote, from … where did you say your home is, Mr Heathcote?"

"Near Winchester," replied Mr Heathcote. He nodded amiably towards Jenny. "I have met your brothers, Mr Henry and Mr Edward Austen. They joined John and me on a hunting party last season."

Jenny's imagination straight away put Mr Heathcote in a red coat, urging his horse to a gallop, the reins in one hand and his crop in the other. It would be an arresting sight, to be sure. "Oh, yes!" she recalled. "When Edward was visiting from Kent. Henry is now in the militia."

"Indeed," said Mr Heathcote, with a small dip of his head.

"William intends to enter the clergy," offered John. "He expects to be ordained within the year."

And is therefore seeking a wife, said Jenny to herself. "Is this your first visit to the Basingstoke Assembly Rooms, Mr Heathcote?" she asked aloud.

"It is, but I am persuaded it will not be my last. My friend John told me of the superior beauty of the girls I would find here, and I must admit he was correct." As he said this his eye caught Catherine's, and she giggled.

"William would willingly dance with all the ladies in the room, if he could," put in John.

But which one will he choose first? wondered Jenny. She took note of William Heathcote's gallantry, and his unembarrassed, unhurried manner. His attentive eyes returned her gaze calmly. His hair was brushed neatly, with no display of fashion, and his clothes were well pressed and simple, like her own. There was a languor, though not an unattractive languor, about him, which Jenny warmed to.

"William must be forever on the move," John Portal informed the ladies good-naturedly. "I simply cannot imagine him composing sermons."

"It is not unusual to enjoy a ball," observed Mr Heathcote. Then he turned purposefully to Jenny. "Are you engaged for the next dance, Miss Austen?"

"No, sir, I am not." Jenny could feel herself blushing. How she hated herself for the sensibility she could not control, especially when a gentleman requested a dance! The ridiculousness of it struck her even as she accepted his invitation. At a ball, what else did she expect gentlemen to do?

"Indeed, who does not enjoy a ball?" agreed Madam Lefroy, looking purposefully between Catherine and John Portal. "Come, shall we circulate?"

Mr Heathcote bowed as they departed, and, while the opportunity presented itself, asked for another dance. "Perhaps the last, Miss Austen? The cotillion, if it pleases you?"

"With pleasure, Mr Heathcote," she replied. "But are you not neglecting the many other young ladies present, who would no doubt like to dance with you?"

His interested expression indicated that she had said something unintentionally coquettish. Her cheeks continued to blaze. Perhaps if he were not quite so handsome, she would be not quite so confused. "That is," she added quickly, "who would like to dance with someone they have not met before. And as you hinted yourself, you would be pleased to make the acquaintance of as many partners as possible."

"I see." He adjusted the white stock at his throat. Not uneasily, Jenny thought. More in the manner of one who feels himself challenged. Why did conversations with young men never follow the scheme her imagination laid down for them? She should have accepted with good grace his apparent desire to attach himself to her. Now, he had been left with no alternative but to indulge in awkward gallantry.

"You must not think my words presumptuous," she began. "I only meant—"

"You meant to be polite," he interrupted. His eyes glittered with something that might have been amusement, or anticipation, or some masculine emotion which Jenny was unqualified to detect. "Until the next dance, then?"

He bowed, and was gone so quickly that Jenny had not time to complete her curtsey. She stood alone for a moment, swallowing her agitation. Then she set off to find the two voices of reason.

Cassandra listened, frowning a small frown. "A Mr Heathcote? From Winchester? Oh, from Hursley Park." Her frown cleared. "I have an idea his father is a baronet. They are very wealthy, Henry says, and Henry always knows how much money people have."

"And this Mr Heathcote has engaged you for *two* dances?" said Martha.

"And *I* received an offer for only one," said Cassandra, pretending envy.

"Is that the gentleman in question?" Martha closed her fan and used it to indicate, as discreetly as possible, William Heathcote being curtseyed to by Mary and Alethea.

"Yes," confirmed Jenny. "How do you like his looks?"

"He is extremely handsome," replied Martha "Let us hope his dancing is as well executed as his features, for your toes' sake, Jenny."

The lines were forming for the dance. Jenny found herself sought out and handed to the set without delay. Mr Heathcote's expression was inscrutable, but as they turned to take their place he remarked, "Madam Lefroy is dancing with her son. Do you not think they look well together? How charming a ball like this is, when friends and relatives can mingle without formality."

Jenny could not immediately reply. The opening bars of the music sounded and she and Mr Heathcote took their first steps. When they had completed the measure she asked him if he often went to balls.

"Not often, perhaps," he replied, pleasantly but without smiling. "But during the London season I do attend some public balls in town, and am occasionally invited to a private one. I must observe that you would not see the range of age and rank evident here at a London ball."

Jenny shrank from making further comment. They danced in silence for some minutes. Unease crept over her. When they had first been introduced she had taken him for a country-dwelling, country-loving man with a background and interests not unlike her own. But now she saw that he was worldlier than that. Like Eliza, he had a house in London and enjoyed the far greater choice of society he could find there.

They had reached the end of the set, and faced each other. "Are you by any chance acquainted with the Comtesse de Feuillide?" she asked.

"I have had the honour of being introduced to her. I believe she is your first cousin?"

"That is correct," said Jenny, taking his hand for the cross-over.

"Are *you* often in town, Miss Austen?" he asked.

"Never," replied Jenny. "London life does not beckon me."

He did not speak. They began the next measure. Jenny's heart was oppressed. She felt herself exposed by her partner's superiority of years, and greater social experience. She must seem to him a simpering youngster, with no claim other than the chance one of blood on Eliza de Feuillide's glittering circle.

The music slowed; they took their positions for the final reverence. "It is a great pity you do not go often to London," he said as he led her back to where Mrs Bigg and

Cassandra sat. "It would be a great pleasure to meet you at the Comtesse's house, or indeed at any other place."

"Thank you, Mr Heathcote, for the dance," she said.

"We are engaged for the cotillion."

"I have not forgotten. Oh!" Jenny remembered. "You have not been introduced to Mrs Bigg. And this is my sister, Miss Cassandra Austen."

Mr Heathcote bowed to both ladies. "I hope your sister will report my performance happily, Miss Austen," he said, bestowing a smile on Cassandra. Then he bowed to Jenny, and walked off.

The evening wore on. Jenny danced with John Portal, who pleased her greatly with his swiftness of foot and lightness of conversation. Then she was asked by Samuel Blackall, a young clergyman attached to the Lefroy party, whom Jenny had met many times, and who achieved neither of these things. But, determined to be pleasant, Jenny found herself accepting another dance from him.

"I can assure you, Miss Austen," he told her in his grave way, "that my asking you for two dances should not be seen as an indication of designs on you beyond that of amicability. I do not wish to align myself unfairly to any young lady at present because, as you have doubtless noted, I am in considerable demand."

"Then I thank you for the favour you bestow upon me, Mr Blackall," said Jenny.

Elizabeth Bigg had not sat down all evening. Mr John Harwood, originator of Elizabeth's confusion at Steventon the previous day, arrived late, but not too late to engage her for most of the remaining dances. Jenny took great pleasure in seeing them together. She had always approved of John

Harwood, a thoughtful man who always took immaculate care of any woman whose welfare he was charged with. His admiration of Elizabeth was evident in every movement of his face, and it was wonderful to see Elizabeth's fair head dipping and turning as they spoke, and his hand gripping hers as they went down the dance. Meanwhile, William Heathcote acquitted himself very elegantly in a Scotch air with an unknown girl in a blue dress, and Jenny danced twice with the energetic Ben Lefroy.

Supper was done, and all but a few scavengers determined to get their full ticket's worth of refreshment had quitted the supper room. The would-be dancers had returned to the ballroom in threes and fours, and the predicted air of relaxation had descended upon the assembly, when Elizabeth Bigg appeared, flushed and bright-eyed, at Jenny's side.

"*He* is here!" she announced in a loud whisper, though the noise was so great that nobody would have heard her had she shouted. "Oh, Jenny, I have waited all my life for him, but at last he has arrived, just when I had given up hope!"

"Who?" asked Jenny, utterly bewildered. "Mr Harwood? But—"

"Do not pretend you are unaware, Jenny, it is too cruel."

"*Cruel?*" Jenny was astonished. "But Elizabeth—"

"You danced with him. I saw you, so do not deny it. And I had to put up with John Lyford! But now he has asked me to dance the last with him."

"Are you speaking of Mr *Heathcote*?" asked Jenny. But he had engaged *her*, much earlier in the evening, for the last dance! Elizabeth had accused her of cruelty, but what could she, Jenny, accuse *him* of? Forgetfulness, or worse?

"Yes, Mr Heathcote!" cried Elizabeth. "Is he not the

most perfect man you have ever seen? I have been speaking to him for the last half hour, in the supper room while the servants were clearing it. He did not mind sitting among the crumbs, because all he wanted to do was look at *me*. Oh, Jenny, when he takes my hand in the cotillion, and everyone is looking at him and thinking how handsome he is, why, I don't know how I shall stop myself shouting with joy!"

"But what about Mr Harwood?" asked Jenny faintly.

"Oh, I have had some dances with him. But, you know, he is not an accomplished dancer, and stepped repeatedly upon my gown. Oh, do not tell me Mr Heathcote dances clumsily! I cannot bear to hear it!"

Jenny's feelings hovered between disappointment for herself, greater disappointment for Mr Harwood, and happiness for Elizabeth, who clearly considered herself to have captured the affections of handsome Mr Heathcote. For his part, the vision of loveliness he saw across the leftovers must have obliterated the memory of the younger, less striking girl who was faithfully saving the last dance for him.

"He dances very well, Elizabeth," Jenny assured her. "And I am quite sure you and he will attract the attention of the whole room."

Elizabeth embraced her impetuously. "What a good friend you are, Jenny! And is it not strange that everything can be going along quite normally, with John This and John That all in their usual places, and then the world stands on its head because a William Somebody has arrived!"

"Most strange," said Jenny, feeling suddenly hot.

The lines were forming for the final dance. Jenny stood alone, struggling for composure. Then three things happened. Out of the corner of her eye she saw John Harwood quit the room, wearing his hat. John Portal led Martha to the set. And Jenny found herself approached by John Lyford. "Are you not engaged for this dance, Miss Austen? I would be honoured if you would bestow—"

"No," she interrupted. "No, I am not engaged, but I do not wish to dance. I thank you, Mr Lyford, but I am very tired, and wish to sit down."

It was not so difficult to refuse after all. Mr Lyford retreated, and Jenny took a seat beside Mrs Bigg. The expression on Jenny's face silenced any questions that lady might have had. With a heavy heart, Jenny watched the flying coat-tails and swirling skirts, the shiny foreheads and blotched cheeks which signified the end of an enjoyable evening. Cass, her hair escaping in tendrils at the nape of her neck, looked extremely pretty as she paraded up the set with Mr Blackall. Mary Lloyd was again dancing with Mr Lefroy, and Catherine with his nephew Ben.

But like everybody in the room, Jenny looked mostly at William Heathcote and Elizabeth Bigg. Though it pained her to think of his conduct towards herself and Elizabeth's towards John Harwood, there was no doubt that they *did* look very beautiful, and very happy, together. Poor John might have arrived at the ball with high hopes of securing a prize, but it was now very publicly clear that he would leave empty-handed.

"Well, Jenny," observed Cass, reappearing during the applause which followed the dance, "I do not recall when I have enjoyed a ball more. If only Tom were here!" She sat down beside Jenny, fanning herself enthusiastically. Then she seized the candle-holder on the table, and drew it nearer her sister's face. "What is the matter?"

"Nothing."

"Jenny…"

"I want to go home," declared Jenny. "Could you encourage Mrs Bigg and the others to make haste? I will tell you all about it tomorrow. Now, I beg you, leave me be."

Cassandra obeyed. But Jenny was aware all the way home in the carriage, while Elizabeth chattered on about William Heathcote, that she was not quite the same Jenny who had left Steventon Rectory earlier that day. She was not at all sure she liked it, but she had taken one more step into whatever it was that lay beyond her cherished childhood world.

BOOK TWO

Betrothed

Elinor and Marianne

The morning after the ball was reserved for discussing it.

"How can a gentleman behave in such an ungentlemanly fashion?" Jenny asked Cass after she had told her sister the story of William Heathcote's defection.

"Quite easily," returned Cass, "if he is not a gentleman at all."

"Do not be so logical! I want an explanation for his behaviour, or, failing that, some words of comfort."

They had slept late, and were taking breakfast upstairs at the little table that usually held their workboxes. Jenny was using her workbox, which had been placed on the floor, as a foot-rest. "You are my older sister and are supposed to be wise about everything that can happen between your age and mine," she said, biting into a slice of toast. "Why did he use me so ill, Cass?"

"I think that sometime after dancing with you, he fell in love with Elizabeth, and everything else went out of his head."

"But he could not possibly have forgotten he had engaged me for the last dance!" Jenny had to put her hand over her mouth to stop pieces of toast falling out in her indignation.

"He *did*," laughed Cass. "And if he could see you now, with butter all over your chin, he would probably congratulate himself on his lucky escape."

"Do not tease, Cass, I am not in the humour for it."

Cassandra took her teacup and went to the window seat. She was wearing her second-best dressing robe, the good one having already been cleaned and packed for Godmersham. "Try not to blame him too much," she advised her sister. "They left the supper room so late, the cotillion was his last chance to dance with Elizabeth. He did not know when he would see her again. Perhaps he never will."

"But what about my prior claim?" protested Jenny.

Cass smiled. "If he thought of it at all, dearest, which I doubt, he probably assumed you would understand."

"Understand? What *can* you mean?"

Cass was still smiling. "However little men know about women, one thing they *do* know is that we tell each other things, especially about them. Usually, he would not have regarded this as an advantage, but last night it was. He knew Elizabeth would tell you that he had secured her for the last dance, and you would be too well-bred to mention that he had done the same with you. Which, you have to admit, you were."

Jenny pondered. "In that case I think his behaviour doubly reprehensible. Not only did he change his mind, but he was too cowardly to admit it to my face."

"Cowardly or clever?" observed Cass. "Anyway, perhaps this morning he feels remorse. Watch the post for the next few days." She put her empty cup back on its saucer. "There. Have I discharged my sisterly duties adequately?"

"More than adequately," said Jenny. "And if he does not write I can blame my disappointment on you, for putting the idea into my head that he might do so."

"But in two days I shall be gone into Kent and will escape your censure."

They were silent for a few minutes. Jenny finished her toast and drank her tea; Cass examined a place on her sleeve where she had mended her robe. Neither girl's thoughts were on what she was doing, but it was Jenny who voiced hers.

"Is it not the case that falling in love has but two outcomes?"

Cassandra's small frown passed over her forehead. Jenny was familiar enough with the small frown to know that her sister's mystification was entirely artless. Cass was incapable of the dissembling and subterfuge Jenny herself indulged in every day. She never dismissed Jenny's hypothesizing, however odd she might secretly consider it. She willingly listened, understood, reasoned and was satisfied.

"The first outcome is that the man does not care for you," continued Jenny. "Result: your heart is broken. The second outcome is that your love is returned. Result: he declares, families are consulted, a marriage takes place, and a life of child-bearing and preserve-making follows."

Cassandra looked at Jenny in surprise. "But what of the *joy* of love? Is it not the most exquisite human experience, which bestows nobility upon even the lowest-minded of individuals?"

Jenny could not help but laugh. "Observe how I am immediately defeated! You see the best in everyone and everything, while I look upon life with a jaded eye."

"Oh, but there is no need," retorted Cassandra with confidence. "Somewhere your future husband waits patiently for you. When you meet him, I predict that every jaded notion you ever had will fly away."

Jenny's affection for her sister rose up. "Dearest Cass, I know you will find great happiness with your Tom. But last night has shown me how powerful falling in love can be. How suddenly it can happen – and how swiftly a woman, or a man, can switch their allegiance. The joy of love, as you so eloquently describe it, is an exquisite human experience, but a precarious one. And we women go through all its passions and problems, thinking of nothing else for years and years of our lives ... for what? For a man who may or may not love us after our youth and beauty have faded away."

"You only say this because you have never been in love," insisted Cass. "You will change your mind, I promise."

"And if I do not succeed in making anyone fall in love with me," went on Jenny, "I shall end an old maid. That is an indisputable fact. But, unlike most old maids, I can at least indulge my habit of writing stories as an alternative to the endless hours of glove-knitting that await me."

"Which reminds me," said Cass, brightening, "we are expected at James's this afternoon. Apparently he and Anne have a gift for me which I am not supposed to know about. Knitted gloves aside, what do you think they have got me which I could possibly want?"

When Mrs Lloyd and her daughters had moved to a small house in the village of Ibthorpe several miles away, the living at Deane had been granted to James. The Lloyds' old house, Deane Parsonage, was larger than the cottage James and Anne had lived in before, with a well-kept garden Jenny had always loved. But Mama considered sitting outdoors, even in early September, detrimental to one's health, so Jenny, her mother and sister, and James and Anne themselves, with baby Anna clinging to her mother's knees, gathered in the parlour. In the Lloyds' day this had been a bright, uncluttered room, always full of flowers. But Anne, who shared her mother-in-law's distrust of fresh air, had closed the windows against it. The room was stifling.

Anne and James were interested to hear an edited description of the previous evening's ball. "I have not been to the Rooms for many years," Anne observed. "James, we must stir ourselves to join the company there again soon."

"Yes, my dear, we must," replied her husband. "Personally, I enjoy dancing."

Jenny saw him gesticulate to Anne, while at the same time pretending he had not done so. When she made no response, he nodded his head towards a cupboard to the side of the chimney breast.

"Oh!" Anne jumped up, surprising little Anna, who sat down unexpectedly hard on the stone floor. The child set up a loud wail. "Cassandra," said Anne, "we have a gift for you. Now, Anna, you are not hurt." Picking her daughter up, she went to the cupboard and removed something wrapped in the sort of paper in which draper's goods came. Shyly, she presented it to her sister-in-law, whose pretence of utter astonishment impressed Jenny.

"What can it be?" wondered Cass, fumbling a little as she opened it. "Oh, a shawl! How beautiful!"

It *was* beautiful. Folded, the shawl took up no more space

than a pocket-handkerchief. Opened out, the delicate, silken-fringed material spread to the size of a tablecloth. Cass fingered the impeccably stitched embroidery. "Anne, you are far, far too kind," she gasped.

"James bought the shawl in London," Anne explained, "but it was plain, except for the fringe. I embroidered it with things you like, Cass. See, here are your lavender plants, and roses, and your beloved pink ribbons."

Cass was moved. "But why…" she began, then hesitated, unsure how to proceed.

James proceeded for her. "We originally thought of it as a wedding gift," he explained, "but when we heard you were to meet Tom at Godmersham, Anne suggested we give it to you now, so that you can wear it while you are there. It is a long time since you have had a new shawl, our mother informs me, and I know that neither you nor Jenny ever asks for anything."

"Oh, thank you, thank you," repeated Cass. "Thank you both."

"Come, try it on," urged James.

Anne helped Cass set the shawl around her shoulders. Cass, pink with pleasure, paraded in the restricted space. "Is it not fine stuff?" she asked, swishing it as she walked. "I can hardly feel it. It is the very best Indian silk. James, you have spent much too much money on me, you know."

Jenny's delight in the gift was tempered by her brother's words. It was true that she and Cass never asked for anything. It was the responsibility of other people to notice their needs and supply them, because they had no money of their own.

It was a timely reminder. Feeling ungrateful and ungenerous, and aware that such feelings would never have occurred to Cassandra, Jenny wondered if anyone would remember when *she* was twenty-one and was going visiting, or collecting her trousseau, that an expensive Indian shawl might be welcome in *her* wardrobe.

How satisfying it must be, she thought, *to have some money, however little, that one has earned oneself!*

"And you shall wear it at Godmersham?" Anne was asking Cass.

"Of course! I am impatient already to show it to Tom."

"You look very well in it, my dear," observed Mama proudly. "If Tom's company makes you as radiant in Kent as you are at this moment, the entire county will flock there to marvel at your beauty. I could not wish for a lovelier daughter."

Anne laughed uneasily. "Are you forgetting Jenny is here?"

"How could I?" Mama looked at Jenny approvingly. "My Jenny has her own beauty."

Jenny decided to take advantage of the public situation and her mother's mellow mood. "When shall *I* visit Kent, Mama?"

Mama paused before she said, "When Cassandra and Tom are married, perhaps."

"But that could be years!" exclaimed Jenny unthinkingly. "I mean, that is…"

"Yes, it could," said Mama. "So in the meantime you must await an invitation from Edward and Elizabeth. It is not for us to make their arrangements for them."

Nobody reminded her that the arrangement for Cassandra to meet Tom at Godmersham had been made by the Reverend. "But, Mama," continued Jenny, "I so wish I could go alone, now I am grown up."

"You are not nineteen yet," said Mama reasonably. "You have plenty of time for parading yourself at Godmersham or any other place. Anne, could I trouble you for a glass of water? I think I shall take a powder; my stomach is weak today. But you know, Jenny, the place I would most like to take you to is not Kent, but Bath. The liveliness of that city never diminishes, however many times one goes there. But Papa does nothing about arranging it."

Jenny had no wish to visit the city of Bath. One brief stay there had convinced her that if "liveliness" meant hot, smelly rooms full of painted women vying with one another to capture the most foppish of the men, she would happily trade them for the "dullness" of Steventon. She disliked cards, rich food made her queasy, and whenever she returned from going about the Bath streets she had to dry her stockings.

"It never stops raining in Bath" she said crossly. "And the puddles are the deepest and dirtiest in the kingdom. James hates it too, do you not, James?"

"It is not my favourite place, I confess." James's approach to differences of opinion between his mother and sisters was always diplomatic. "But it has some advantages, not least the number of balls held there. And do not deny you like balls, Jenny."

"There you are, miss!" cried Mama. "And even if you do not go to Bath or Kent, we have plenty of balls nearer home for you to attend. The Biggs will hold a Christmas ball at Manydown this year, as they always do."

"Christmas! Mama, it is only September."

"Christmas will come soon enough," said Mama. "Which reminds me, I must pick those last raspberries tomorrow, before the birds have them all, and Travers and I can make jam. You can help us, Jenny, while Cass is away."

Anne brought the glass of water; Mama's weak stomach was placated; James read from a book of sermons; they played with Anna before she went to bed. Walking home in the calm, cooling air, with the scents of berry bushes, grass and horse-manure all around, Jenny sensed her sister's pensive mood and took her arm.

"What shall I do for five weeks without you, Cass?" she asked softly.

"Survive perfectly well, you little goose."

Jenny was quite prepared to spill her feelings in letters, but letters were no substitute for the security of her sister's presence and her good advice. The puzzle of William Heathcote had not seemed so complicated to Cass. She had concluded something entirely reasonable and communicated it to Jenny in well-chosen words, soothing her sister's fevered emotions.

My sensibility, thought Jenny, *and Cassandra's sense.*

While Cass was making ready for bed, Jenny sat at the writing desk. Under the blotter lay the manuscript she had been so secretive about. "A reflection of ourselves," she had told Cassandra. In her mind she had the story of two sisters, whose different dispositions led them into interesting situations. She even had their names, the prettiest she knew. But not until this moment had it been clear which of them was which, and why they were so different. Now, she knew.

Taking the pen, she dipped it into the ink and wrote upon a fresh sheet: *Elinor – sense. Marianne – sensibility.* Satisfied, she laid down the pen. Tomorrow she would start *Elinor and Marianne* in earnest.

Henry

$\mathcal{A}$s Mama had forecast, Christmas came soon enough. Jenny's nineteenth birthday was followed by a yuletide season so cold that Steventon Rectory became Cassandra and Jenny's prison. The sisters were overjoyed that both Henry and Frank, their naval officer brother, had obtained leave for Christmas. But the snow was too deep for the carriage to get to Manydown House for the Biggs' traditional Christmas ball, and neither the sisters nor their brothers could go.

It was partly this disappointment which prompted Mama and Papa to procure a spring invitation from Edward and Elizabeth in Kent. But Jenny was not to stay there alone; she was to be accompanied by Cassandra and Henry. *Patience, Jenny*, she told herself. *Only two more years until you are of age.*

Much as she had looked forward to the Biggs' ball, Jenny's enthusiasm had been dampened by the possibility that William Heathcote would be there. Elizabeth Bigg had kept the neighbourhood on tenterhooks for the past few months by maintaining a ladylike silence on the subject of the handsome clergyman. To Jenny, Cass, Martha and Mary she had confided, with tears, that now he had taken orders and had obtained a living even further away than Winchester. Moreover, her father was not sure that he was a wealthy enough suitor for her.

"But he is the son of a baronet!" Mary had protested.

"That is true, my dear Mary, but he is the *younger* son. He will inherit neither the title nor the land. And he may have forgotten all about me by now," Elizabeth had added pathetically, beginning to weep again. "I have not seen him for so long, I sometimes wonder if I should even hope that he will ever declare his intentions, whether to me or to my father."

"Meanwhile," Martha had suggested, "you have other suitors, do you not?"

"Oh, yes. There is always the devoted John Harwood. I suppose I had better not absolutely spurn his attentions, because he definitely *will* inherit. Though less, of course, than Mr Heathcote's elder brother."

Jenny had had to rein in her indignation at this guileless cruelty. Kind and pleasant as her friend was, and however much in love with William Heathcote she declared herself to be, Jenny understood that any girl endowed with beauty such as Elizabeth's liked to count her suitors in units of more than one, and would never marry a penniless man.

But the thought of meeting Mr Heathcote again worried Jenny nevertheless. No note of apology had ever come. Would he regret his conduct and be embarrassed when he saw her? Or worse, would he simply have forgotten he had ever danced with Miss Austen of Steventon?

When the snow put paid to the ball Jenny's nerves settled. But then Edward and Elizabeth invited the sisters for a visit which was to include a week spent with Eliza in

London. If Mr Heathcote was indeed acquainted with their cousin he might very well visit her while Henry, whom he also knew, was in London too. After so many months without a word, Jenny might have to meet him again under the scrutiny of Eliza, Cass, Henry and half of London society. Meanwhile, Elizabeth Bigg and her scrupulous father would be many miles away in Hampshire.

Cassandra knew her sister well. "You must not think they are sending me as chaperone, you know," she said gently, watching Jenny put the manuscript of *Elinor and Marianne*, which Cassandra still had not been permitted to read, into the bottom of the heaviest trunk. "Our sister-in-law Elizabeth will chaperone both of us."

"Elizabeth will do no such thing," replied Jenny. "She will not accompany us to Orchard Street, that is for certain. Henry has been recruited for that duty." She began to rearrange the trunk's contents, the better to hide the string-bound pile of papers.

"Henry will not object to it," observed Cass. "You know how much he enjoys going into London society. And Eliza's house is always full of people ready to admire a young man in uniform."

"Exactly," said Jenny, with feeling, "yet Mama will not allow me to go there, or even to Godmersham, with Henry alone. Someday you shall be free of me, Cass. Though I shall expect a warm welcome in the household of the Reverend and Mrs Tom Fowle whenever I decide to visit."

Cassandra was quiet for a few moments. When she spoke there was strain in her voice. "Do you think I *wish* to be free of you?"

"Why, Cass!" cried Jenny in dismay, sitting back on her heels. "I only meant that someday you shall be married, and no longer living here. You know no one loves you as well as I do! We shall be the very best of friends for ever!"

Cass, unable to suppress sudden tears, went into the bedroom and closed the door. Jenny did not follow her; she knew her sister wanted to unravel her thoughts by herself. But it was rare to see Cassandra in distress. Could the length of her engagement, now almost three years, be less bearable than she advertised to the world?

Jenny wished she had not spoken. Why had she not seen that this visit to Kent would be for Cass a poignant reminder of last September's visit with Tom? She decided she must make it up to her sister. She had meant it from her heart when she said that no one loved Cass as well as she did; Tom's was surely a different kind of love. She went to the bedroom door. No sound came from within.

"May I bring you anything?" she called softly, without opening the door.

Cass's voice sounded the same as usual. "No, thank you, dear. But you might tell Mama that I shall not be taking dinner today. I have no appetite."

Jenny nibbled her thumbnail. It seemed she had been summarily dismissed. But, fired with a new determination to consider her sister's feelings, she went to deliver the message.

"Oh, Lord!" were Mama's words. "She is not going to be ill, is she, when everything is planned for tomorrow? Does she look feverish?"

"Not in the least," Jenny replied. "She merely has no appetite, and wishes to spend a quiet evening before a long journey."

Mama, though she would never *wish* any of her family to be ill, dearly loved to have an invalid on her hands. "We shall see how she is in the morning," she declared. "She shall not travel if I consider her unfit to do so."

Henry, lolling in an armchair, exchanged a secret smile with Jenny. "If Cass has to stay at home, may I still take my other sister on the visit she has looked forward to for so long?"

"Certainly not," returned Mama. "I would not trust *you* to take care of the strapping of a trunk, let alone the chaperoning of a nineteen-year-old girl."

"Unfair!" protested Henry.

"Perfectly fair," retorted Mama.

When her mother had gone to see about the dinner, Jenny took the rare chance of a private conversation with Henry. There were things, important to her if not to him, that she had long wished to ask him about.

"Henry, do you remember William Heathcote?" she began. "He has been hunting, he says, with you and Edward. I believe he lives at a place called Hursley Park, which is ... I do not know where it is."

The words came out so hard upon each other that Jenny was not sure her brother had understood. But after a moment's thought he turned to her. His countenance, normally so open, was inscrutable. "Yes, I know Heathcote."

"He is a suitor of Elizabeth Bigg."

"Ah. Along with half the county, I would wager."

He shifted in his seat, adjusting his waistcoat. Then he fell to a careful inspection of his boots.

"Cass and I met him at the Assembly Rooms last September," Jenny told him. "He said he knew Eliza. I wondered if you had met him at Orchard Street."

"As proof that he truly *does* know Eliza?" asked Henry.

Jenny was startled at the sharpness of his tone. "No, I do not think so. I suppose I want to know your impression of him, that is all."

"And of his suitability for you, Jenny Wren?"

Childhood resentment flooded back, exacerbated by her intense affection for Henry. "Do not call me Jenny Wren," she told him frostily. "My name is *Jane*. I merely want to know what you think Mr Heathcote is like."

"Has he committed some offence, that he requires a character witness in order to please you?"

"Not at all. I shall tell you what happened, since it is no secret. He was very attentive to me. He asked me for two dances. But then he saw Elizabeth Bigg." She watched while Henry dusted the knees of his breeches. "However, I dare say I am asking the wrong person. Men do not concern themselves with such things."

"I assure you, men do."

"Then what do you know of him?"

"He is rich, though not the inheritor of the estate. He is to take orders, I understand."

"He already has."

Henry shrugged. "I *have* met him at Eliza's, and from my own observation, he is attentive to the ladies."

"So are you, but let that pass."

"His understanding is good," he declared, "and his manners are gentlemanly."

"I agree. And his person?"

He shrugged again. "He rides well, and is a handsome devil, as I am sure you are well aware. Are you in love with him?"

"No!" said Jenny, knowing she was flushing, but not caring

because Henry was treating the matter seriously. She asked him her most important question. "Do you think he will be invited to Orchard Street while we are there?"

He rested his elbow on the arm of his chair and leaned his chin on his hand, half hiding his face. When he spoke again, his voice was weary. "Do not quiz me any more, Jenny. I am sick of the man."

"So if I *were* inclined to fall in love with him, you would counsel me against it?"

"No more quizzing!" he pleaded. "And since counsel will never defeat love – have you ever known anyone be *persuaded* out of their affection? – I will say nothing."

Godmersham's beauty was quite different from that of Steventon, but the smoothness of the lawns, the grandeur of the chestnut trees holding up their white candles, the pleasant situation of the house and the glorious aspect from every window impressed Jenny profoundly. For the hundredth time, she marvelled at Edward's luck.

Of course, his luck was partly due to his own charm. He had not James's authority nor Henry's good looks; Frank was a formidably able officer, and Charles was the most light-hearted of all the Austen brothers. But Edward possessed qualities which had brought him wealth beyond anything his brothers could hope for. Generous and loving, as a child he had taken the fancy of Mr and Mrs Knight, distant relatives of his father. Having a large fortune but no children of their own, when Edward was still a young boy they had asked to adopt him legally, as their own son and heir. His parents, knowing that his alternative prospects were narrower than those the Knights were offering him, had readily agreed to this proposal. Upon Mr Thomas Knight's death, Mrs Knight had moved into a smaller house and left Edward and his wife Elizabeth installed at Godmersham Park.

"I am not sure I like our sister-in-law's practice of calling me 'Aunt Jenny' in front of little Fanny," said Jenny in a low voice. "The child is bound to do the same."

They had been at Godmersham for three weeks. It was the first truly warm day of the year, and Jenny and Cass were walking in the park, preceded by Elizabeth, who was hand in hand with two-year-old Fanny. Behind them, talking animatedly, strolled Henry and Edward.

"I am resigned to 'Jenny' from my elders," continued Jenny, twirling her parasol, "but from small children it is an impertinence of the first order."

"Tell Elizabeth she must refer to you as 'Aunt Jane', then," suggested Cassandra.

"*You* tell her."

Cassandra laughed. "Whatever little Fanny, or little Anna for that matter, chooses to call you, you will accept," said Cass. "You are as indulgent towards our nieces as I am."

"Then shall I tell them to call you 'Aunt Cassikins'?"

"Jenny, these stays are too tight to laugh in!"

"In that case you had better not wear them tomorrow. Eliza's parties are always full of jokers, and I do *not* mean on the card tables."

Cassandra's face straightened. "Oh, *cards*, and the kind of dinner that takes half an hour to spread out, while the food gets cold. And elegant young ladies playing the piano. No, the harp."

"And singing, but since Eliza is still in mourning, no dancing," added Jenny. "However, if Eliza wants to invite us to those grown-up sort of parties, you know we must go, Cass." She gave an exaggerated sigh. "Dear me, such a lot to complain about when one has a social whirl like ours! But it will be good to see Eliza again."

"Whenever I feel nervous and stupid, which I often do before Eliza, you are always there to make me smile again," said Cass warmly. "Who will perform this office when Tom and I are married, and you are far away?"

"No one will need to, because married women do not feel nervous and stupid, of course," replied Jenny without hesitation.

A raised voice behind them made both sisters stop and turn. Edward and Henry were walking towards them. "Ladies, what do you say to a carriage ride?" asked Edward. "Henry has prevailed upon me to transport him to Canterbury this afternoon, from where he intends to take the public coach to Dover. "

"Dover?" Cassandra addressed Henry in surprise. "Why are you going there?"

"I have someone to meet."

"Off a ship?" asked Jenny eagerly. "From France? Who is it?"

"Suffice it to say that Henry is going to Dover," said Edward with finality. "Now, would you like to go with him as far as Canterbury, or shall our nonsensical brother complete his entire journey alone?"

"I would like to go," said Jenny, "if we may travel in an open carriage. Is it a warm enough day for the barouche, do you think?"

"I believe so," Edward told her, smiling. "It will be a pleasant outing for us all."

"And I shall travel back from Dover tomorrow," said Henry.

"Tomorrow!" echoed Jenny in dismay. "Have you forgotten that we are going to Eliza's tomorrow?"

"I shall try to join you at Orchard Street later in the evening."

"But…" Cassandra was bewildered. "Mama said you were to escort us there."

"My man Craven shall accompany you on the journey," put in Edward, with a glance at Henry. "He is a good man; he has served at Godmersham for fifteen years."

Much as Jenny loved Henry, she could not help but feel dissatisfied with this turn of events. "Are you not disappointed," she asked, watching his face, "to be missing Eliza's party?"

Henry set off across the grass, walking more quickly than before. "No, I am not disappointed. I attend our cousin's parties whenever she invites me."

"From Petersfield?"

"Petersfield is no distance from London. And Trident knows a good gallop when he sniffs it."

"And he gallops back?"

"The next day, yes."

Jenny wanted to ask more questions, but the familiar suspicion that some questions were unacceptable had descended upon her, and she remained silent. She wished she knew what was in Henry's head. But why should he tell her? Younger sisters were there to be taken for carriage rides, and be satisfied.

She was quiet at luncheon. But once they had left Fanny in the arms of her nurse and, with much waving and blowing of kisses, had climbed into the barouche, her spirits lifted. Four young horses, eager for the exercise, were driven by Edward's coachman at a fast pace towards the Canterbury road. Blossom-scented April air rushed past Jenny's cheeks, tearing her curls from beneath her bonnet and whisking them into her eyes. She blinked and gasped with exhilaration. Cassandra was laughing, full of the same excitement, and Henry laughed too, at the sight of his sisters enjoying themselves.

"You two will be the centre of attention tomorrow night," he predicted.

"What excuse shall we make to Eliza for your absence?" Jenny asked him. "If you wish, I could say your regiment has been called to action at short notice, and that you sailed on the first packet out of Dover to join your men."

"A romantic notion," said Henry affectionately. "Make it into a story. But I have written to Eliza. I do not expect my sisters to make my excuses."

William Heathcote was not there. The card players, the girl with the harp, and the array of carefully arranged dishes were all present, but once all the guests were assembled, and no black-clad clergyman had made an appearance, Jenny's nerves ceased to be jangled with every opening of the front door.

"Eliza must be the only woman in London who can make mourning look so glorious," she whispered to her sister.

"When she leaves off her mourning clothes," said Cassandra, "I predict her first gown will be gold. Look at all these ladies in gold. It must be this season's colour."

"Do you think she has remembered her promise to take us to a ball?"

"I am confident she has," said Cassandra. "But Tom and

Charles are supposed to accompany us, if you recall. Eliza is determined to procure that double wedding."

"Determined she may be," said Jenny, "but once and for all, Cass, I do *not* intend to marry your future brother-in-law."

Supper was over. The music was about to begin. Eliza gathered her guests in the most beautiful room in the house. Jenny, who had made only one previous visit to Orchard Street, several years ago when Hastings was a baby, remembered this room well. It was not as large as the drawing-room, but it was classically proportioned, with French windows giving onto a balcony. Its faultless decoration and highly polished floor reflected the efforts of a large staff dedicated to the comfort of their mistress.

As she sat down on an upholstered chair of the highest quality, Jenny pictured the drawing-room at Steventon: its casement windows and the inglenook Papa refused to dismantle despite its old-fashioned appearance. *I am lucky to sit amid luxury, here and at Godmersham,* she said to herself as the harpist prepared to begin, *but how many girls can go home and sit cosily in an inglenook as well?*

During the applause which followed the first song, Eliza sat down on the empty chair next to Jenny. "I have not had a moment to speak to you, my dear," she said. "Are you well? You look different. Older, I suppose. And wiser, do I detect?"

Jenny could only reply to this with a lowered gaze.

"But equally beautiful," concluded Eliza.

"Cassandra is the beautiful one. But, yes, I am well."

"Cassandra looks more careworn than I remember."

"She wishes she could be married, I suspect."

Eliza sighed. "If I were in her shoes I would have eloped long ago."

"She and Tom would never elope!" Jenny was shocked. "Imagine what it would do to Papa!"

"I speak in jest, my dear," Eliza assured her. "Though people *do* elope. Sometimes it is their only choice."

"But does it ever result in happiness?"

"That depends on the participants and the circumstances. If a couple truly love each other, and there is no objection other than social, or financial, on the parents' part, why should love not triumph over prudence?"

"You sound like Henry," laughed Jenny, flipping open her fan. It was becoming hot as more guests, attracted by the sound of music, strolled in and took seats.

"Henry?" repeated Eliza blankly.

"Why, yes. He told me once that in his view, counsel never defeats love. Is that not exactly the same sentiment as you have just expressed?"

The harpist began; Eliza was not obliged to reply. Jenny listened to the song. The playing was brilliant, and the programme impressive in both taste and execution. Jenny's own efforts to sing were dismal by comparison. When it was over, she turned to ask Eliza the young lady's name, but the chair next to her was once more empty.

She did not see her cousin again until the company was dispersing. Eliza, a well-practised hostess, lingered in the hall with her guests. Jenny leaned over the banisters outside the drawing-room, watching her. The light from the chandelier fell on her jewels, subdued though they were, and her dark, brilliant eyes. Yes, Cassandra was right. Jenny could see Eliza dressed all in gold.

"*There* you are!" Cassandra came out of the drawing-room followed by an elderly couple. "Lord and Lady Portsmouth wish to take their leave of you."

Jenny and Cass accompanied these old friends down the steps and spoke to them while their cloaks were being brought. Each sister received a compliment on her looks from Lady Portsmouth, who had not seen either of them for over a year. Lord Portsmouth, flushed from Eliza's plentiful wine, told Cass that he thought Mr Fowle was a lucky man, and that Miss Jane would also "catch a good 'un". Amused, Jenny saw them to their waiting carriage, kissed Lady Portsmouth and promised to visit soon, then waved to them as the carriage pulled away.

It was when she had half ascended the flight of steps to Eliza's front door that Jenny heard the sound of another carriage stopping outside the house. A young man jumped down from the carriage without bothering with the step, as young men will. He was wearing his hat, and it was dark, but Jenny could see it was her brother Henry.

He paid the driver and started up the steps. He was about to take off his hat, but when he saw her he stopped, and left it on. In his eyes she saw an odd, almost feverish glow. She was about to greet him, but to her surprise he grasped her wrist and put his finger to his lips.

"Jenny, I beg you, be silent. Listen to me. Go back into the house now, and do not tell anyone that you have seen me."

"Why?"

"Do not let Eliza, or Cass, or anyone else, know I was here. Will you promise?"

"Very well." Jenny did not know what else to say. Though his face was shadowed she could see enough of it to be alarmed by the intensity of his expression, and the tightness of his grip on her arm.

"I am indebted to you," he said. Then he spun on the ball of his foot as if ordered to do so by his commanding officer, bounded back down the steps and made off into the darkness of the street.

Jenny did not sleep that night. She lay in the dark for a long time, with Cassandra's regular breathing a background to the scenes which revolved in her wide-awake brain.

Henry had promised to "try and join them later", and had arrived in time to do so. So why did he change his mind about entering the house when he saw her? If she had not been there, it was clear he would have continued up the steps. She could only conclude that he had expected the party to be over earlier. He had expected his sisters to be in bed, and the house in darkness.

Beside her Cassandra stirred, flailing an arm which struck Jenny's shoulder. Jenny gently returned the arm to her sister's side, thinking, thinking…

When Cassandra had settled again Jenny fumbled for the candle-holder by the bed. Feeling her way to the desk, she lit the candle. The flame showed her that Eliza's housemaid had tidied the desk that morning: the pen holder, the inkstand, the blotter were all in their places, and the pen-wipers had been replaced.

Elinor and Marianne lay in her trunk. Stealthily she took the manuscript out and placed it before her on the desk. She chose a pen and loaded it with ink. A drip fell on the manuscript. She blotted it slowly, watching her fingers turn the page over and back again, frowning and thinking.

Her encounter with Henry had given her another glimpse into the complications of other people's lives. She was quite sure that he had been in pursuit of something when he alighted from the carriage. It could not be a woman – surely if he had wanted to meet women he would have attended the party. So what was it?

A new idea stabbed her heart, but she made herself consider it. What was the other thing men pursued endlessly, apart from women? Money. Always money, as Eliza had told her over another candle flame, on another sleepless night. Henry had no money, Eliza had a great deal. Could he be borrowing from her? Could her brother be in debt to his cousin?

Jenny tried to think. *Men's motives are many, and often obscure*, she told herself. *Mama always maintains that Henry would rather say anything than own the truth, and this is an excellent indication of how fathomless are the depths of his private business.*

Somewhere in this evening's events lay the resolution of *Elinor and Marianne*, for which she had been searching for weeks and weeks. It was hidden amid Henry's secretiveness and her own suspicion that his behaviour had its origin in financial concerns. She chewed the end of the pen, thinking, thinking…

Marianne and Elinor must both suffer from someone else's secrecy. The point of the story was, after all, to show the two sisters' different ways of braving the world's disappointments. Marianne's lover must marry someone else for money, and Elinor's must be separated from her by a youthful indiscretion. *Women and money, money and women*, she said to herself. *It is the way of the world.*

She found a fresh piece of paper and replenished her ink, which had dried by now. Slowly at first, then faster, she filled page, then another. Then she sat back and chewed the pen for a few moments, and began to write again.

"Jenny! What are you doing?"

Cassandra had awoken, alarmed. She began to get out of bed, her braided hair swinging. "Is something amiss?"

Elinor, Marianne and their lovers disappeared into the desk drawer. Jenny picked up the candle. "Do not stir yourself. I could not sleep, that is all."

"Are you unwell?"

"Not at all." Jenny got back into her side of the bed and pulled the covers up. "I could not stop thinking about my story. I had to get up and write down my thoughts before I forgot them. Now, let us both go to sleep, or I shall be fit for nothing in the morning."

"You may sleep late," said Cassandra, already drowsy again. "There are no chores to do at Eliza's."

But neither sister was able to sleep late. The church clock at the corner of the street had barely struck six when Jenny awoke to find Eliza at the bedside. Looking gravely beautiful in a silk house-gown, with her hair still in curling papers, she shook Cassandra awake. Jenny hoisted herself up on her elbows. "Whatever has happened?"

"A letter has come by express post," explained Eliza. "You are both to return to Godmersham at once. From there Henry will take you back to Steventon."

"What is it?" whispered Cassandra.

"It is your sister-in-law."

"*Elizabeth?*" Cassandra put her hand to her throat.

"No – James's wife, Anne" said Eliza. "Yesterday evening…" She caught her breath. Her voice began to shake; she would soon be in tears. "Suddenly she was struck by some sort of seizure, and died."

Cassandra gave a small shriek and collapsed against her sister. Upon the foot of the bed lay the silk shawl Anne had embroidered for her only a few weeks ago.

"Our poor dear James witnessed it all," said Eliza. She gripped Jenny's hand. "I cannot stop thinking of that precious child, Anna. To lose one's mother at two years old! Oh, my dears, how frivolous and stupid my little party seems now!"

Two Toms

"Here is a piece of news for you, Miss Jenny," said Mama, looking meaningfully over the top of her spectacles. "His mother writes here that Charles Fowle has gone off to London, to study at the Inns of Court, after which he expects to be called to the Bar."

It was December, the month in which Jenny's birthday fell. This year's, her twentieth, had been spent without Cassandra, who was spending Christmas at her future in-laws' house in Berkshire and would not be back until Tom had embarked on a new chapter in his life, a journey to the West Indies. The winter was as cold as the previous one, when they had been prevented from attending the Christmas ball at Manydown House. Mama had insisted Jenny quit the upstairs sitting-room and sit with her by the drawing-room fire.

"You are still not quite well from that little fever you had," she had said briskly, "and if you start coughing, there will be no stopping you all winter. Anyway, with a two-year-old living in the house there is no time for writing.

Come along, Aunt Jane."

So Jenny had unwillingly laid down her pen, wrapped herself in her thickest shawl, and was now sitting in the inglenook, watching the fire.

"Mrs Fowle seems very pleased that Charles is going to be a lawyer," said Mama. She consulted the letter again, then laid it in her lap. "Now, Jenny, what profession would you have predicted that he would follow? I must confess that when he was a boy I always rather saw him as a soldier."

"I remember that he used to march around with a stick over his shoulder for a rifle," said Jenny. "But then, if you recall, my own favourite pastime at that age was playing with model animals, yet now I have no inclination even to own a pet cat."

Her mother was not listening. She had bent down to attend to Anna's latest request. "No, you cannot have my scissors, precious one, you are too little. Where is Baby? Did you leave her upstairs?"

Baby, a beloved doll, had been squashed behind a sofa cushion earlier that morning by an excited Anna, entranced by Kitty's cleaning of the drawing-room. Following the maid about with a hand-brush had amused her greatly, but only for half an hour.

"There is nothing for the child to do," observed Mama, retrieving the doll. "You and Cass always had each other, and when Charles was a baby he and Frank were inseparable. But a child alone... No, Anna, you *cannot* have my scissors. Think of something, Jenny!"

"I looked after her all day yesterday and have no more ideas."

"Is that so?" Mama was exasperated. "What is amiss with you this morning?"

"Nothing, except that I am not quite well, as you have already told me. I would like to rest."

"So *I* am the one to run around after Anna today, am I?"

"Mama, I was with her all day—"

"Yesterday. So you said. Well, when you have your own child, you will be its mother *every* day. I only hope your future husband will have funds enough for a good nursemaid."

With an effort Jenny retained her patience. "Mama, I did not mean to sound selfish. But with Cass away my reserves of invention are under strain. Much as I love Anna, and however good a child she is, sometimes I need my sister to help me with her."

Jenny's mother took Anna on her lap. "Come, you sit up here with grandmama, and we shall nurse Baby. Shall you sing her a lullaby, to help her go to sleep?" Her eyes darted towards her daughter "Speaking of future husbands, how much do you think a lawyer earns these days?"

"Oh, Mama, *please!*" pleaded Jenny, though she was relieved to see the mischief on her mother's face. Sometimes, and this morning seemed to be one of those times, she struggled to avoid losing Mama's favour, and however momentary the loss, she was always very glad to get it back. "May I speak of future husbands too?" she asked. "What do you suppose Tom is saying to Cassandra at this very minute?"

"That is not for our ears, Jenny."

"But we know he is wishing her goodbye."

"Very likely," agreed Mama. Anna's head lay against her grandmama's breast. The child had dropped Baby onto the floor, and her chin had sunk onto her chest. Mama stroked her granddaughter's hair. "Very likely," she repeated softly.

Jenny knew that Mama was picturing the scene as vividly as she herself could see it. There was Cass in her bonnet and cloak, smiling bravely in the icy wind as Tom threw his pack onto the roof of the coach. Jenny knew exactly how he would look, holding his hat on with one hand and clutching his pocket-book in the other. He would stoop from his lanky height and kiss Cass's cheek, and his mother's. Then he would shake his father's hand and climb up after his pack. Thrifty to the last, he would sit outside with the driver in all weathers.

"Tom will have left home by now," observed Jenny. "He is on his way to Falmouth to wait for his ship to sail. Falmouth is in Cornwall, is it not?"

"It was the last time I looked at a map," said Mama, still caressing her grandchild. The child's eyes were closing. "Mrs Fowle mentions in her letter that he has a hard few weeks ahead of him; but the Fowles are all very proud of him for volunteering like this. And so should we be."

Cass had confided to Jenny the strongest reason for Tom's deciding to be an army chaplain and sail to the West Indies with his regiment. The colonel had offered Tom a better living when the expedition was over. *A large house and garden, with a stable and dairy,* Cassandra had written from the Reverend and Mrs Fowle's home. *It is in Shropshire, a village parish within jaunting distance of Shrewsbury. What could be more perfect? Tom is apprehensive about going to the West Indies, but he is prepared to do it in order to secure our future together. Oh, Jenny, I wish I had your talent for writing, so that I could express on paper how dearly I love him!*

But Jenny had not communicated Cassandra's words to Mama. With no sign of the war abating, she could not cause her mother further anxiety by telling her that the date of Cassandra's wedding, and indeed her future security, depended upon Tom Fowle's success with the regiment. But it was a commission he had little inclination for, and it might be dangerous into the bargain.

Instead, she drew the shawl closer around her shoulders and said, "We *are* proud, Mama. And we shall add him to the list of soldiers and sailors we pray for every night."

Mama gathered the almost-sleeping Anna into her arms and rose carefully. "Jenny, my dear, you are not aware of this, since I take care to hide it so well. But I live on my nerves, wondering every day if bad news will come. And although Henry is safe at the University for the present, when he has finished his degree he will have to go back to the militia. Our dear Frank is still at sea, and Charles – dear God, Jenny, he is only sixteen! – will soon follow. Yes, we who are left behind can only 'stand and wait', as the poet says." She indicated with her head for Jenny to open the door. "And, by the way," she added as Jenny did so, "the invitation from the Biggs came today. The Manydown ball is to take place two weeks after Christmas, while Cass is still at the Fowles'. But I take it *you* wish to go, snow permitting…"

It was strange, attending a ball without Cassandra. And it was cold in the carriage, clad in evening dress in January. Jenny grasped her fan and the little beaded evening bag Martha Lloyd had lent her, feeling nervous though she knew she should not. She would be among friends, and she was already among relatives. James sat opposite her in the carriage and Henry by her side.

James smiled indulgently whenever she caught his eye. "You look very well tonight," he told her. "Does she not, Henry?"

Henry was always kind, but not always careful of his words. "Yes, indeed. And without Cassandra at her side, perhaps our youngest sister will be noticed rather more than usual?"

"I would rather Cass *were* here," confessed Jenny.

Manydown looked glorious. On their latest visit to Steventon, Alethea and Catherine Bigg had described with great excitement how they had persuaded their father to decorate the house more extravagantly than usual. "You will be all astonishment," Alethea had predicted. "Fairyland will be a very poor second!"

Jenny was not sure that the version of fairyland in *her* head could ever be a very poor second to anything, but when Henry handed her down from the carriage she gasped. The house blazed like a bonfire, with flickering chandeliers visible in the ballroom, and upstairs curtains draped back to reveal illuminations in all the windows. Flares bedecked the garden too, and even the greenhouse was lit so brightly it no longer looked like a greenhouse, but a transparent palace worthy of the grandest of princesses.

"Here are the Austens!"

A female voice, which turned out to belong to Elizabeth Bigg, and the scarcely less high-pitched one of her fifteen-year-old brother, mingled in greeting.

Elizabeth was very excited. "Mama and Papa are in the hall, but Harris and I cannot help coming out to see people's astonishment when they arrive. The house looks wonderful, does it not? Do you not think we have a generous papa!"

"You do indeed," observed James. "What the final account will be for all this I cannot imagine. Or rather, I can!"

Amid the laughter this caused, Elizabeth took Jenny's arm and led her towards the house. "Because the snow made last year's ball such a disappointment, we wanted to do something special, you see. And we have so many young gentlemen! Madam Lefroy has brought her nephew, and all "the Johns" are here."

"John Lyford, John Portal and – am I correct? – John *Harwood*?"

"And who, pray, is John Harwood?" asked Elizabeth archly.

"Oh, Elizabeth…"

"All right." Elizabeth lowered her voice. "Yes, John Harwood is here. But so is William Heathcote. I fear tonight may be the last occasion upon which poor Mr Harwood will count himself a suitor… Why, Jenny, what is the matter?"

Jenny had stopped a few paces short of the front door. "Elizabeth, tell me once and for all," she demanded, "has your father changed his mind? Do you intend to accept William Heathcote if he should speak tonight?"

"I do. And no, my father has not changed his mind. I have changed it for him."

Jenny looked earnestly at her friend, but saw no trace of embarrassment on her face. She tried to think. If William Heathcote was here as Elizabeth's probable future husband, she, Jenny, must act as if nothing had happened. His conduct must be the guide of hers.

"He has already asked me for the first dance," Elizabeth was saying airily, "and I expect I shall dance with few other men all evening, except out of politeness."

They had reached the ballroom. "Look about you, Jenny," invited Elizabeth. "Is it not splendid? All the usual collection of acquaintance is here. The Lloyds – is that not Martha's reticule, with the beads, by the way? It matches your gown beautifully. And all the Lefroys and their friend Mr Blackall and … oh, there is William, waiting for me."

William Heathcote approached, bowed to both ladies and held out his hand for Elizabeth's. At the lowest point of her curtsey, Jenny looked up at him, but he was not looking at her. His smile was only for Elizabeth.

As Jenny straightened up, however, courtesy demanded he acknowledge her. "How pleasant to see you again, Miss Austen," he declared in his reserved way, quite at his ease.

"And you, Mr Heathcote. My brother Henry, whom I believe you know, is also here tonight."

"Splendid!" He smiled broadly. "Shall you do me the honour of dancing with me later?"

"Of course, if you wish. The cotillion, perhaps?" suggested Jenny.

Mr Heathcote and Elizabeth exchanged looks.

"Ah," said Jenny. "The 'Shrewsbury Lasses' then?"

He bowed. "I have very happy memories of doing that delightful dance with you at Basingstoke, and look forward to repeating the pleasure."

In the eighteen months since Jenny had last seen him, William Heathcote had become, if anything, more attractive. Indeed, Jenny found herself almost shocked by the unembarrassed pleasure both he and Elizabeth took in their own beauty. Now that he was master of his own house, his languorous manner had become a satisfied air. He radiated bonhomie, and was evidently not inclined to spoil it by resurrecting old oversights. Not even his unadorned clergyman's clothes could detract from the impression of height, strength and elegance his figure gave. Elizabeth, despite her eighteen months of uncertainty, had truly done well for herself.

Jenny watched them begin the dance. Then, remembering that she was standing alone in a ballroom, she lowered her shoulders, held up her head and tried to smile. Suddenly, she found herself surrounded by Madam Lefroy and her sons, Ben and George.

"Miss Jenny!" came Madam Lefroy's familiar cry. "And your brothers are here too, I notice. What is keeping your sister from the company? Is she not yet returned from Berkshire? But how delightful to see Mr James venturing out! And how does his little daughter fare at Steventon? Are her aunts enchanted with her still?"

Which question do I answer first? wondered Jenny. But a curtsey seemed all that was required of her, because Madam Lefroy immediately began speaking again.

"You know, do you not, my dear, that our good friend Mr Blackall has spent Christmas with us? He is now a Fellow of Emmanuel College, in Cambridge, and has recently been ordained. He was looking for you a little while ago. I believe he has something *very particular* to ask you. Such a bright young man!"

"Certainly, ma'am," said Jenny. It was difficult not to be uncomfortably aware of Madam Lefroy's ceaseless attentions to the prospects of young people. She did not desire the attentions of Samuel Blackall, but she would at least please Madam by dancing with him. His conversation might be heavy, but his feet were light.

"I am going up to Emmanuel next Michaelmas," said Ben importantly.

"Mr Blackall has secured a living – a good one, I assure

you, my dear," continued Madam Lefroy, "and we would like to help him broaden his circle of acquaintance, particularly with young ladies."

"Oh, do take him off our hands," cut in George Lefroy impatiently. "The Reverend what's-his-name has been at our house for three days and we need somebody else to talk to him."

"Sshh, George!" Madam Lefroy waved her fan gaily. "Why, here is Mr Blackall now!"

The Reverend Samuel Blackall, Fellow of Emmanuel or not, looked the same as he always had. The large head on narrow shoulders was still there, and the reluctance to look at his interlocutor's face. His manner had become haughtier since Jenny had last seen him, and his tendency to nod his head unnecessarily had increased.

"How pleasant to see you again, Mr Blackall," said Jenny, making him an elegant curtsey. "I trust you are well?"

"Very well, I thank you, Miss Austen," he said, nodding.

She wondered what *very particular* thing he could have to ask her. He was not at his ease, that much was clear. Perhaps he was aware of Madam Lefroy's throwing them together, and would rather it had happened more naturally. As soon as he began his next speech, however, Jenny began to doubt this.

"My honoured friends," he said, indicating Madam Lefroy and her sons, who were exchanging resigned looks, "have bestowed their most excellent hospitality upon me this Christmas while my new home is being made ready for me. I have secured a living, you see, in Dorset."

"A pleasant county, by all accounts," said Jenny, "and not so far away as to render visits to your old friends difficult."

"Indeed, Miss Austen," he replied stiffly, with a small bow.

Samuel Blackall's elevation in education had not been accompanied by any elevation in wit. Jenny searched her head for social platitudes of the sort that came so easily to Cassandra. What had her sister advised her once? When in tedious company, speak of books.

"When you are established in your own house, Mr Blackall," she began, "perhaps you will embark upon the collecting of a library – though I cannot foresee many libraries surpassing the one at Ashe, of which the Reverend Lefroy is justly proud."

Mr Blackall's reply was sagacious, and so lengthy that Madam Lefroy, her smile faltering, was obliged to interrupt it. "Mr Blackall, did you not have something very interesting to put to Miss Austen? You must say it before the dancing begins, since it is never advisable to speak of serious subjects while dancing. I believe you wish to ask Miss Jane about her writing? Such delightful stories, so clever and comic!"

The young clergyman shifted from one foot to the other. He did not look at Jenny.

"Do you read novels, Mr Blackall?" she asked, by way of a prompt. "You know, stories of family life, or adventure, or mystery?"

"Actually…" Still he did not look at her, but his eyes rested upon her right ear, in which she wore one of her best earrings, of silver and amber. Jenny wondered whether the size of his head was exaggerated by the large – nay, enormous – wing collar he wore. Was this some Cambridge fashion? "Actually, my interest in novels is extensive, and it is upon that subject that I wish to address you. Of course, as a clergy-man I have read widely in every field."

"Of course."

"Literacy, I believe, is the way forward for civilization. To that end, I am introducing in my new parish a school for village children. People of that sort will, of course, never read philosophy, or science, or history. It is as much as we can do to instill the Scripture into them. But if they were to be provided with suitable reading material in the form of novels, I believe that as much can be learned from such works as any other."

Thinking of Kitty's admission of her acquaintance with Mrs Radcliffe's books, Jenny could only approve. "I applaud your venture, Mr Blackall, and wish your parishioners many years of novel-reading."

He had gone very pink, and where his light brown, rather unkempt hair met his brow, beads of perspiration had appeared. "Thank you, Miss Austen." At last he looked at her, his flush deepening. "Indeed, since you speak so agreeably of my scheme, might I prevail upon you to listen to a proposal I have long nurtured, but which I have not had the opportunity to air until this moment?"

Jenny did not dare look at either of the Lefroy boys. "A proposal? Of course."

"I have the outline of a story concerning a young clergyman," Mr Blackall announced. "It contains a modicum of personal experience, of course, but I flatter myself I have made the character sufficiently unlike myself as to be unrecognizable to my friends."

He stuck his thumbs into his waistcoat pockets. For one panic-stricken moment Jenny thought he was going to produce the "outline" from one of them. "I wonder, Miss

Austen, if you would do me the honour of allowing me to send it to you, so that you may peruse it and perhaps use it for your next book?"

"Mr Blackall, I am most gratified—"

"A novel," he continued without noticing Jenny had spoken, "with a strong religious theme, which avoids the sensational elements in many modern books which *masquerade* as novels, while all the while being the devil's work, must be considered to provide for the lower orders reading matter both instructive and godly. Do you not agree, Miss Austen?"

"Wholeheartedly," said Jenny. Helplessness had descended upon her; she put up her fan and coughed discreetly behind it. "Pray tell me, sir, why do you not write this novel yourself?"

His face, still red from embarrassment, reddened further from some other emotion. "Novel-writing, Miss Austen, is perfectly acceptable as a pastime for young ladies such as yourself. But please do not intimate that *any* novel can be serious enough to bring anything but *mortal punishment* upon a member of the clergy!"

Madam Lefroy came to Jenny's rescue by hurriedly instructing her sons. "Ben, take Mr Blackall and fetch us all some punch. And you, George, find your cousin Tom and bring him to me *immediately*."

When they had gone she turned back to Jenny with a gleaming eye. "Mr Blackall is not the only young person whose company I have secured this evening. My nephew, Mr Thomas Lefroy, has come over from Ireland and is also staying at Ashe this Christmas. Mrs Bigg kindly extended her invitation to him, and I always maintain that the more gentlemen we can bring into the company of our young ladies the better."

Jenny's spirits sank. Her smile fixed itself to her face, but it was not sincere. She did not wish to be a chesspiece in Madame Lefroy's matchmaking game. The Reverend Blackall's shortcomings she knew well enough. But she had not bargained with trying to think of amusing things to say to yet *another* protégé of the well-meaning lady. She would greet this nephew, and make her excuses as soon as was polite.

George reappeared, holding his cousin's coat-sleeve. He delivered him to Madam Lefroy with a bow, then went to join Harris Bigg, who was sliding on the polished floor in his stockings.

Jenny noticed that Tom Lefroy had reddish hair and light, cheerful eyes, and that there was something familiar about him.

"Tom, my dear, this is Miss Jane Austen, of Steventon," announced his aunt. "I have mentioned her to you, of course."

Tom Lefroy made a swift, rather nervous bow, which brought his forelock over his eyes. With an equally swift movement he pushed it back. "Delighted to meet you, Miss Austen."

"Mr Lefroy," said Jenny as she curtseyed.

"I understand you were introduced to my father at Basingstoke," he said.

"Oh…" said Jenny. "Why, yes, I was." Of course, this Mr Lefroy must be the son of the Irishman who had so charmed Cass at the Assembly Rooms ball.

Ben returned bearing glass cups on a tray. The Reverend Blackall was nowhere to be seen. Tom Lefroy took two of the cups. "Punch, Miss Austen?"

"Yes, please."

It was churlish to refuse. And besides, he was looking at her with a mock-grave expression which communicated his awareness of his aunt's intentions.

"Let us take some punch to Papa," suggested Madam Lefroy to her son, pulling him away by his coat-tails.

Jenny sipped her punch. It was as warm as the room and very sweet. She remembered to smile at Mr Lefroy, but her nervousness had risen the instant his relatives had departed. Fearing that he would think she was fishing for a partner, she surveyed the room with an air of studied nonchalance. Her gaze fell on Elizabeth Bigg, whose beautiful eyes followed William Heathcote's every movement; the rest of her face was obscured by her spread fan. Suspecting that her own smile must seem false, Jenny decided to put up her own fan. But it was dangling inelegantly from the wrist which held the punch cup. She transferred the cup hurriedly to the other hand, spilling some of the liquid on her glove as she did so.

"Oh! No matter, these are old gloves. That is, not *old*, but..."

For the first time since they were introduced, he smiled.

To her shame, Jenny felt her heart leap. Tom Lefroy's smile affected his face so entirely that the eyes, cheekbones, lips and teeth suddenly appeared to her quite changed. Sweetened, yet still masculine. She had never seen any man look like this before. Was it his air, the set of his shoulders, the darkness of his evening dress against the lightness of his colouring? She was looking at a man who attracted her as no other man – even William Heathcote – had ever done.

Should she be thinking such things? It was schoolgirls' nonsense, of course. Tom Lefroy would turn out to be either too worldly or not worldly enough, too talkative or too quiet, too eager or too reticent. He would be unintelligent, or drink too much, or be interested only in hunting. He might be as boring as John Lyford. Most probable of all, he would not like her.

"Will you do me the honour of dancing with me, Miss Austen?" he asked, looking expectantly into her face.

She felt none of the embarrassment requests for dances usually produced, and accepted as calmly as if one of her brothers had asked her. But when Tom Lefroy led her out onto the floor her heart felt as if something heavy were pressing it. She could not feel her legs at all. She executed the steps without knowing it, aware only of how naturally her hand fitted into her partner's, and how unreservedly delighted he showed himself to be whenever she caught him looking at her.

After the dance he did not let go of her hand, make a correct bow and seek his next partner, as gentlemen usually did. He conducted her to a chair at the side of the room and, flipping his coat-tails, sat down next to her.

"Sitting out" together, when they had only just met! Why, Jenny was behaving more impulsively even than Elizabeth, whose dance with William Heathcote had been followed by their huddling in a corner, as familiarly as if they were already engaged. Jenny remembered Elizabeth's flushed, almost hysterical appearance at Basingstoke, when she and Mr Heathcote had merely spoken in the deserted supper room. Now, after one dance with Tom Lefroy, could Jenny honestly say she was any less enraptured?

"So you have … let me see, six brothers?" Tom Lefroy was saying. "And one sister? And is she still at home?"

"My sister Cassandra is engaged to a Mr Tom Fowle, and hopes to be married when he has returned from military service overseas."

"Tom! A name I heartily approve of!" he said, his face consumed by the beautiful smile.

Jenny lowered her gaze modestly. If she went on looking at him, she was sure that her own smile would break the bounds of her cheeks and leap around the room, rejoicing in its freedom as gleefully as she now rejoiced in Tom Lefroy's company. "Indeed," she said. "Thomas is not an unusual name."

"Do any of your brothers possess it?"

"No."

"What are their names, then? My aunt has told me, but I confess my ears were more alert to *your* name than any masculine one. Tell me about them."

He was flirting with her. It made her feel like she had often imagined Cassandra felt in the presence of *her* Tom. Strong, at peace with the world, secure in mind and person.

"First is James," she began, "who is a clergyman. He has the living at Deane, the very next village to Steventon. His little daughter lives with us because his wife died eight months ago. In fact, he is here tonight." Her eyes roamed over the dancers. "There he is, dancing with Miss Catherine Bigg. Next is Edward, who is married and lives in Kent, then Henry, who is at Oxford at present but is soon to rejoin his regiment in the militia. He is also here, though I cannot see him dancing. Then Francis – we call him Frank – and Charles, who are both serving in the navy."

He pondered. "That is five brothers," he said with uncertainty. "Am I to conclude…"

"Oh, no!" corrected Jenny. "That was remiss of me. Our other brother, George, who is between James and Edward in age, is unwell and must be cared for away from home. He is ever in our thoughts and prayers."

"And your father is a clergyman, I understand?"

"Yes, and he also has a school in the Rectory. Only a few boys, but it sometimes seems as if there are…"

"…several hundred?" he finished for her. "It must feel a little crowded." His light eyes were full of the pleasure Jenny knew he could see in her darker ones. She and this most amiable Irishman were understanding each other.

"Exactly so," she told him. "But you must live in a large house, Mr Lefroy, which does not have a school in it. Therefore you are surely a stranger to such concerns."

"Not at all. My father owns land, but our house is not as large as Ashe. And now you must guess how many brothers I have."

"I guess four."

"Guess again."

"Five?"

He shook his head. The forelock fell over his brow again. Jenny watched his fingers as he pushed it back. His hands were square-palmed, with broad knuckles like Papa's. Her heart began to gallop. Would there ever come a day when Papa would invite this man into his study, and close the door behind them, and… *Stop*, she reprimanded herself.

"I have no brothers at all." He sat back in his chair. The expression on his face showed some envy, but there was also an element of apology in it.

"But you have sisters?" she ventured.

"Three."

"I see."

"My mother is confident she can marry them all to suitable husbands."

"If she cannot, your aunt will!" Jenny declared, laughing.

For a moment she thought she had offended him. It *was* a rather impertinent remark. But his surprise was instantly replaced by delight, and he shouted with laughter, so loudly that the guests seated nearby turned to see what the commotion was.

"I envy your brothers," he told her when he had recovered his composure. "None of my sisters ever says anything to make me laugh." He leaned forward again; his face was only inches from hers. "But truly, I am very, very glad that you are *not* my sister."

Jenny could not reply. This was more than flirtation. He had hinted as plainly as possible what propriety decreed he could not say outright. Her blood rose; she felt hot, and highly conscious that she and Tom Lefroy were being watched by several onlookers.

"How warm it is in here!" she cried, fanning herself. "Why does someone not open a window?"

"On a cold night such as this, I suppose it would not be advisable," he replied reasonably. He looked steadily at her for a minute. Though her face blazed, she no longer felt self-conscious. Indeed, she *wanted* him to look at her.

"You have very handsome eyes, Miss Austen," he said.

"Thank you." She was tempted to return the compliment, but stopped herself. Elizabeth Bigg would never tell William Heathcote to his face how good-looking he was, and Jenny could not have had a better teacher in matters of courtship.

"Have you ever had your portrait taken?" he asked.

"No. That is, not officially. I sometimes sit for my sister as her model for sketching."

"And are her sketches like?"

"Sometimes."

"Do you also sketch, Miss Austen?"

"I do, but I am not very good at it."

"What pursuits do you follow during your spare hours, then, if I may enquire?"

Jenny smiled. It was easy to behave attractively, secure in the knowledge that she *was* attractive to this man. However she looked, he wanted to look at her. Whatever she said, his attention was chained. "Like all young ladies, I sew, play the pianoforte and sing." She dipped her head and raised her eyelids as she had seen Elizabeth do. "I am learning French and German, and I improve my mind with serious reading. But unlike other young ladies, I am not at all talented at any of these things."

Tom Lefroy's returning smile was wider even than Jenny's own. "I refuse to believe you are without talent. My aunt certainly does not think so."

"Do you mean your aunt has spilled my secret?"

His smile faltered. "Oh! I was not aware that…"

"Do not make yourself anxious that you have betrayed her," Jenny reassured him, putting up her fan to hide her amusement at his discomfiture. In fact, his lack of guile was recommending him very strongly to her. "It is no secret that I write stories."

"My aunt learnt from your mother that you have completed a novel. Is that true?"

"Do you ever answer questions, Mr Lefroy, or only ask them?"

"I will tell you on one condition," he returned, his composure once more intact. "That you cease addressing me as Mr Lefroy, and call me Tom."

"In that case, I too have a condition. You must call me Jane before I disclose any more about myself."

"Very well, then. I am asking so many questions because I want to find out as much about you as I can in the short time available to us at this ball. I cannot monopolize you for the whole evening, as I am persuaded several other gentlemen would very much like to dance with you, and so you must forgive this catechism I am subjecting you to. Do you forgive it, Miss – I mean, Jane?"

Jenny laughed "I do, Tom. And, yes, it is true that I have written a novel. A real, three-volume novel."

"You are very young to have completed such a feat," he said admiringly. "It is as much as I, or my sisters for that matter, can do to write a letter."

"Writing comes to me as easily as breathing," said Jenny. "And if I were prevented from writing, just as if I were prevented from breathing, I would die."

She had never confessed this to anyone, even Cassandra. After she had said it to Tom Lefroy, she felt as if they had set foot together on territory no one had explored before. Mindful of Cass's advice about speaking of books in tedious company, she pushed the thought aside and addressed Tom eagerly. "Do you like reading novels?"

He paused. "I am not familiar with many," he said carefully. Clearly, he was anxious not to offend her, but was equally anxious not to tell an untruth. "I began *Tom Jones*, but I must confess I never finished it. In our house novels seem to be the province of ladies."

"Diplomatically put!" laughed Jenny. "Ladies read them, and ladies write them. What could be more fitting? Cassandra will be delighted to hear it when I tell her. She is a great reader of novels."

"When she is not sketching?" he asked good-humouredly.

"Indeed. Nor sewing, which she is very good at, or playing the piano and singing, or—"

"Improving her mind with serious reading?"

They both laughed. Jenny knew without any doubt whatsoever that this was the happiest she had ever been. As their laughter subsided, Tom inclined his head closer to hers. "Do you tell you sister everything?" he asked.

"No," replied Jenny truthfully. "She is my confidante, and I am hers, but we both have things we do not share."

"In that case, please do not tell her that we have allowed ourselves to address each other by our first names. I wish it to be between *us*."

He said this with a look of such boyish, and therefore very charming, embarrassment, she could not possibly refuse.

"Very well, Tom, it is."

He took her hand. "And now, Jane, do you hear the music beginning again? Do you want to dance?"

As they walked to the set, Jenny could feel herself glowing – with pride, with happiness, with the secure knowledge that she was admired. She determined to savour every moment of the evening as if it were her last on earth, in order to relate it all, with the exception of the part she must not disclose, to Cassandra.

James, Henry and Eliza

$\mathcal{T}$om Lefroy was to return to Ireland in two weeks. When he and his young cousin George made the customary visit to Steventon the day after the ball, the call was brief even by duty-driven standards. Jenny barely had the chance to address him; each time she looked at him his attention was elsewhere. But on the way out of the garden gate he turned and ran back, hat in hand, to where she stood on the doorstep.

"Pray do not forget, Miss Austen, that you are cordially invited to my uncle and aunt's ball at Ashe next Friday. May I engage you now for the first dance?"

"Certainly, Mr Lefroy," she replied, and they smiled at each other.

Bundling up her skirts in the way she used to when she was a little girl, Jenny climbed the stairs three at a time. Huddled in her shawl, with mittens half-covering her hands, she now wandered about the cold sitting-room, thinking, thinking…

In the corner of the writing desk was the little pile of

cross-stitched pen-wipers Cassandra had made for Edward years ago. Faded now, but still serviceable, they were as much a part of the familiar surroundings of Steventon as the carved chair Jenny now pulled out from under the desk, and the embroidered cushion on which she sat.

The sight of her sister's handiwork drove all thought of story-writing from her mind. What flowed from her pen was a letter to Cassandra. A long, long letter. By the time Jenny had finished her hand ached and weariness had begun to overwhelm her. She was also, she noticed, weak from hunger. She had been too nervous to eat breakfast.

Tiptoeing down to the kitchen, she begged some bread and cold meat from Travers. Then she carried her spoils back upstairs, settled herself upon the bed and gave herself up to the dreams that Mama called "nonsense". It was not nonsense, though. Jenny preferred to think of it as writing her own story instead of someone else's.

She was twenty years old, the very age Cassandra had been when she became engaged to *her* Tom. Jenny's own Tom (she could permit herself to think of him as that in dreams) was twenty-three, that perfect age between majority and marriage that she envied Cassandra for possessing. How extraordinary it was, that just as one Tom was leaving for the West Indies, another Tom had appeared from Ireland. Jenny had to concede that the first country was rather less exotic than the latter; but one's own story was never as exciting as fiction, after all.

"Nothing can diminish my happiness," she said aloud, licking her fingers. "I *know* he likes me. This is what Marianne felt when that scoundrel Willoughby courted her, and Elinor when she fell in love with Edward Ferrars."

She sat up. Should she look over the manuscript of *Elinor and Marianne*? Now it had happened to *her*, should she revise the passages about falling in love, in case the real feeling was different from the one she had described?

She lay back, nestling among the pillows, and smiled to herself. No, she would not. *Elinor and Marianne* was finished and done with. And who was to say she would have leisure enough in future to dwell on the prospects of those fictional sisters anyway? Her own prospects had suddenly begun to diverge radically from the life of an author.

In church the next day Jenny heard neither Papa's words nor the congregation's responses. Her prayers were private. *Please, please, God,* she asked, *watch over Tom Lefroy and keep him safe from harm. Do not separate us in spirit, even when we are separated by distance. And please send me the wit to make him laugh, because I cannot live without seeing his smile again.*

The Lefroys' ball would be the test of Tom Lefroy's allegiance. If he remained constant in his pursuit of her, there would be no avoiding the embarrassment of public exposure. If not, she must make certain that neither her words nor her countenance betrayed any attachment to him.

Monday went by very slowly. By Tuesday morning Jenny was on the point of asking, in desperation, if Mama had any letters for the post, or messages for anyone in the village. Taking them would be an excuse to get out of the house. Despite the cold weather, she could dawdle up the lane without having to hide her ungovernable excitement from anybody. But as she approached the drawing-room the sound of a horse made her open the front door. A footman, his boots and coat thrust hurriedly over his Ashe livery, put a letter into her hand. "Miss Austen? From Mr Lefroy. Good day to you, Miss."

Jenny tore the letter open. Tom, in a flowing though not particularly legible hand, repeated his request for the first dance on Friday evening and added that, though they must not risk impropriety or, worse still, his aunt's all-seeing eyes, he would very much like to dance as many of the other dances with her as he possibly could.

He signed himself *Your friend, T. L. Lefroy*, but as Jenny pored eagerly over the words they assumed a deeper meaning. What else could he call himself but her friend? Yet, as everyone knew, friendship was the first step to love. She was sure that he was thinking of declaring his feelings at the ball. From declaration to proposal was another short step, which she could reasonably expect him to take before his return to Ireland. And then...

She replied in kind – a succinct, friendly, encouraging note – then she wrote a much longer letter to her sister. At the post office she found an equally thick one awaiting her.

Dearest Jenny, wrote Cassandra, *Tom Lefroy is obviously perfect for you. I am wild to meet him, to see if you have indeed caught "a good 'un", as Lord Portsmouth so quaintly put it. Meanwhile, my Tom has reached Lisbon, from where I have received assurances that he is in good health, not seasick anymore, only sunburned. Write to me immediately after the Lefroys' ball, will you not?*

Jenny hid this letter, and hoped Cassandra would do the same with those she had received. She took great care not to bring Tom's name into conversation with Papa or Mama, and especially Henry, whose penetrating intelligence she did not trust to remain insensible of the powerful impression the Irishman had made.

But keeping such a secret was not easy. A casual reference to the Manydown Christmas ball would burn Jenny's ears and dry her mouth. She could not even make a suitable reply when Papa remarked one evening how numerous were these Lefroys, adding that he wondered if by the time the Revolution was over England would contain more Frenchmen than France did.

Tom Lefroy, however, appeared to be less successful than Jenny at affecting nonchalance.

"What is this we hear from Madam Lefroy?" asked Mama at dinner on Wednesday. "She tells me her ball could see the continuation of an 'understanding', as she described it, which exists between you and one of her nephews, whose name I believe is Thomas."

Jenny looked at her plate. She felt Papa's look; she hoped he was smiling.

"I could neither confirm nor deny Madam Lefroy's report," continued Mama, "because I have heard nothing about it from my own daughter. She, however, has seen plenty in the demeanour of her nephew to indicate an attachment. What do you say, Miss Jenny?"

"Peace, my dear," said Papa to Mama. "Jenny met Mr Lefroy last Friday for the first time. He is surely no more than an acquaintance."

Jenny signalled her gratitude by pressing his foot with hers under the table. But Mama was not to be denied.

"An acquaintance?" she said pointedly. "An acquaintance would not sit out with Jenny for *four* dances, leaving other young ladies short of a partner. *And* looking like a man who has lost sixpence and found a sovereign, according to Madam Lefroy's account."

"Which may be questionable," observed Papa.

Jenny knew she must speak. "I do like him, Mama," she said, blushing. "He is very gentlemanly and pleasant."

"And handsome, his aunt says," said Mama, her eyes watching Jenny keenly, alert to any clue.

"Anyone would say that about their own nephew, however plain he actually was," declared Papa.

"He *is* handsome, Papa," said Jenny. "But it is not his features which make him so; it is his expression." She turned to her mother. "You never saw such kind eyes, and so merry a smile."

Her parents exchanged looks. "Thank Providence that Henry is not here," said Papa dryly. "He would not forbear to quiz you more closely than your mama, you may be sure."

"So am I to conclude that you have hopes of this Mr Thomas Lefroy?" inquired Mama seriously.

Jenny nodded, half embarrassed, half relieved.

"Then we had better get out that pink gown Cassandra had for her first ball at Godmersham," said Mama. "Kitty can sponge and press it, and as you are a little taller than your sister I shall sew on new trim." With a glance at her husband, she added, "And I think, Miss *Jane*, you are old enough now to wear my wedding pearls, which will handsomely set off the pink silk and your brown hair."

Steventon, 16 January

Dearest, dearest Cass,
Oh, how I wish you were here! When do you intend to return? I am glad of Tom F's good health, but I must confess to a certain difficulty at present in thinking about any man other than Tom L.

His attentions to me last night at the ball left me in no doubt that he entertains a serious attachment to me, though he did not absolutely declare. As for me, I suspected when we sat out at Manydown that I might grow to love him, but now I know, Cass, that I do love him, very dearly. There! I have written it. If you are wondering what to do with this letter when you have read it, here is my recommendation: if I never see Tom again after he quits Ashe on Thursday, burn it and never remind me of it. But if I settle in Ireland as Mrs Tom Lefroy I give you permission to keep it, and let me read it again when we are old ladies (and the Two Toms are old gentlemen).

Did you feel like this when you fell in love? I do not remember your betrayal of any excitement, or joy, though I am sure you must have felt it. You are so expert at hiding your feelings, I am persuaded that even that paragon of patience, Miss Elinor Dashwood, cannot outdo you.

You ask me what I intend to do with Elinor and Marianne; *the answer is that I do not know. How does one go about finding out whether one's work is suitable for publication? So far, having shown the book only to you, and read part of it aloud to Papa and Mama, I have only my family's unreliable praise to rely on. Furthermore, whenever I finish a story I am impatient to be writing another, rendering the previous one unimportant. So you see I am lost in confusion, and would far rather gain pleasure from writing than money from publishing.*

Please, please write to me when you next have leisure to do so, and tell me how a well-bred young lady behaves when she is in love. Each day until Thursday I shall be expecting a visit from him. He must come to take his leave of me on Wednesday evening, must he not, out of common politeness? Will he declare then, do you suppose? Will he ask to see

Papa in his study? Oh, Cass! If he does not, quite frankly, I fear I shall die. In which case, my dear sister, I bequeath the fate of our friends Elinor and Marianne to your capable administration.

Meanwhile, I remain your wretched sister, who will spend the next five days loitering near doors and windows, straining to catch sight of my Irish friend coming down the lane. You may picture me, if you care to, and laugh.

With warmest regards,

J. A.

Sunday, Monday and Tuesday passed with no visit. Jenny decided that family matters had kept Tom too busy to call, and she would have to settle for a note. Her head began to ache from the strain of listening for a cantering horse and a knock on the door. On Tuesday night her dreams were filled with visions of Tom Lefroy riding down the Ashe road wearing a footman's livery with his coat and boots over it.

Wednesday arrived, but Tom Lefroy did not. On Thursday Jenny dressed herself more than usually carefully and sat down with her sewing in the inglenook. Kitty brought the letters at midday; nothing from Ashe. The afternoon passed; no visitors. By bedtime, Jenny's light-hearted prophecy that if Tom did not declare she would die had darkened into sinful thoughts. She heartily wished herself dead.

If only Papa and Mama, and the entire Lefroy family, even Ben and George, were not aware of her disappointment! She could have borne it better in secret. But at the Ashe ball, Tom's preference for Jenny had undoubtedly been noticed. The first and the last dance, and several in between, had belonged to him. Between dances, and at supper, they had sat together. And when he had helped her into the carriage at the end of the evening he had brushed her hand with his lips so affectingly that she could not suppress her agitation all the way home. Madam Lefroy, who had been wishing guests good-night close by, had seen this.

To have her parents pity her was almost more than she could countenance. Their efforts to raise Jenny's spirits, kindly meant, met with failure. And to make everything worse, at the very moment when she most needed her sister, Cass was not there.

No letter came from Ireland. After two weeks, Jenny ceased to look for one. Each day she rose and stood before the looking-glass, regarding solemnly her pale face and swollen eyelids. She bathed her face in cold water and tried her best to cultivate an inscrutable demeanour. She smiled as she went about the village with pattens over her shoes as usual. If anyone had pressed her, she might have admitted that she was avoiding visiting Ashe or Manydown for the time being, especially since the weather was so inclement. But nobody did.

The name of Tom Lefroy passed Papa's lips only when he told Jenny that a chance meeting with Reverend Lefroy in Basingstoke High Street had confirmed that Tom had indeed arrived back in Ireland, and was not expected back at Ashe for some time. Mama did not mention him at all. Even James, who had been present at both balls, seemed to have forgotten Tom's existence, while Henry, the greatest gossip in Hampshire, was back in Petersfield and oblivious to everything.

But Jenny could not forget Tom's laughter, and the sincerity in his soft Irish voice. How could she discount his bashful efforts to secure the first dance, the note brought by the footman, his interest in her writing, his admiration of her eyes? Given his own choice, even if he was not ready to declare his intentions at the Ashe ball, he would have visited her the next day, written to her again, taken a tender leave of her when he returned to Ireland. In short, he would have wooed her.

She was sure, she was *absolutely sure* that he had been prevented from pursuing her by outside forces. As the only son in a wealthy family, the responsibility of making an advantageous marriage lay upon Tom Lefroy as much as upon his sisters. Unlike Jenny's brothers, he was not expected to make his way in the world in order to support a wife and family. He must finance his future by means of a union with another landowning family. Jenny remembered how his family situation was the very first thing he had told her about himself, and his questions to her had been on the subject of her own. Money had been uppermost in his mind even then.

My stupidity is second only to my vanity, Jenny confessed bitterly to herself. *How could I have imagined that he might forego his obligations for the daughter of a clergyman? I know Eliza's words about money conquering love to be true, so why did I let Tom Lefroy's smile drive them from my head?*

She had learnt a hard lesson. In the middle of yet another tearful night, she made the decision to leave real-life love alone for a while and go back to fictional love, over which she had control. As she had confided to Tom during that dizzying first conversation, she could not help writing any more than she could help breathing. And when she was writing, she could not think about Tom's smile.

January passed. The beech twigs that tapped Jenny's window

became studded with buds, then the bright spring leaves unfurled. Each day she bent over the writing desk. By the time Cassandra came back from Berkshire with a letter from the West Indies in her pocket, and Eliza arrived for her first visit to Steventon since the death of her husband, the bones of a new book lay in the drawer.

"You see, Cass, there are two young men," explained Jenny, who was kneeling on the bed, clutching one of Cassandra's petticoats, which she was supposed to be folding. Kitty had gone down to help Mrs Travers, and the bedroom was strewn with unpacked clothes and empty trunks. "One of them is very rich, very grand and proud, and the other is amiable and easily led. The pleasant one falls in love with a girl who has no fortune, and she falls in love with him. But his rich friend persuades him that she does not care for him, and they part."

Abandoning the petticoat, Jenny jumped off the bed, ran into the sitting-room and sat at the writing desk. Through the doorway, she watched her sister eagerly. "And then, you see, the proud man falls in love with the penniless girl's equally penniless sister, so deeply that he decides to propose to her. But of course, after the way he has treated her sister…"

"…she refuses him!" concluded Cassandra, laying her best gloves carefully in paper. "My dearest Jenny, that is a delightful idea. And do you have a title for the book yet?"

"Perhaps *First Impressions*? Because in the end the proud man and the girl who refuses him *do* marry, having revised their opinions of each other."

"And do the amiable one and his beloved marry too?"

"Of course! Have you ever known my stories not to end

happily? The world has too much sorrow, without my adding to it in fiction."

"Am I to keep *First Impressions* to myself, as nobly as I kept *Elinor and Marianne*?" asked Cassandra. "Or has your confidence increased sufficiently for Mama and Papa to hear of it?"

Jenny pondered. "Yes, they may," she said at last. "But Cass, would you refrain from mentioning it until after Eliza is gone?"

Cassandra did not ask why. She understood Jenny's reluctance to discuss the new book before their cousin. Cassandra herself had often suffered as self-consciously as her sister under Eliza's enthusiastic scrutiny, complimentary though it always was.

"Of course," she said. Entering the sitting-room, she paused, looking at her sister carefully. Then, in a tone of great tenderness, she spoke again. "Now, tell me, dearest Jenny. Is there any news from, or about, our Irish friend?"

Jenny hesitated. "No. I no longer hope for any."

"Then … if you still wish it," continued Cassandra, her voice still at its most gentle, "should we burn the letters?"

Tears leapt to Jenny's eyes; she could only nod.

Cass reached into the bottom of her trunk and retrieved a ribbon-tied bundle. Meanwhile, Jenny, blinking and sniffing, separated Cass's most recent letters from the pile in the writing desk. "Oh, dear!" she exclaimed, in an attempt to cover her confusion, "the one I wrote to you about the Two Toms is especially mortifying. Yours are much more circumspect."

"Do not punish yourself," returned her sister. "We are all beyond rational behaviour when we are in love. One day I might ask you to burn the letters I wrote to you when I was staying at Godmersham with *my* Tom."

"If you do, I shall disobey, since there is nothing in them to warrant such destruction," returned Jenny. She rose, and poked the fire so vigorously that a storm of sparks landed in the hearth. "I shall throw your letters on before mine, if you do not mind."

First to meet its death was Cassandra's letter about Lord Portsmouth and the "good 'un". Then Jenny threw her sister's other letters after it, holding the burning paper down with the poker. The sisters knelt by the fire and watched the letters blacken and twist, and become ashes.

"Now it is your turn," said Jenny. A sensation surged through her as she said the words, though she could not name it. Loss? Wretchedness? Guilt, that she had committed to paper a premature conviction that she would be cherished for ever by the man she loved?

"Do you want to look at any of them, one last time?" asked Cassandra gently.

"No! Do not torture me!"

"Very well." Cass untied the ribbon around the letters and dropped the first one into the flames.

Tears splashed down onto Jenny's gown. She wiped her eyes with the back of her hand. "Oh, Cass, I do not know how I shall ever get over this."

The letter lay in the ashes. Cass took the poker and pushed it nearer the flames. "You will get over it with the help of those who love you."

"But the agony of not being able to mention him to anyone is unbearable!" wailed Jenny. "I cannot bear never to see him again, yet if he ever comes back into this country, how shall I bear a meeting with him?"

Cassandra took her sister into her arms. "Jenny, your

heart may be broken, but at least you do not have the pain of suspecting his attentions were merely frivolous. We both know that he was sincere, and his desertion of you was engineered by other hands."

Jenny's tears flowed, wetting Cass's cheek and neck, but she made no move to wipe them away. At last, when Jenny could speak, it was to observe that the whole affair, however miserable, had at least left her the legacy of the idea for a book. "Tom is like Mr Bingley, the easily led young man in *First Impressions*," she told her sister. "And the other one, Mr Darcy, is like Madam Lefroy, seeking to separate a pair of lovers on the pretext that the woman does not return the man's love. But they are both wrong, Cass!"

Late afternoon became early evening; Kitty came in to light the candles. The shadows darkened and the sky began to show its stars. Cassandra continued silently with her unpacking while Jenny sat beside the hearth, looking into the fire as intently as if she hoped to make the burnt letters magically whole again

"I had better go downstairs, Jenny," said Cass at length. "I have been up here for hours, and Mama will want me to tell her all the Fowles' news. And Eliza is here. I ought to speak to her too."

Jenny nodded. She was calm, but her face felt stiff and her muscles weary. "You go, Cass," she said. "I shall sleep soon."

"Very well. Goodnight."

But as Cassandra opened the door, Eliza appeared at the top of the stairs. She looked odd – not quite distressed, but flustered, with pink cheeks and bright eyes. "May I come in and warm myself?" she asked, darting into the room. "My fingers are freezing."

Jenny rose from the hearth, confused, knowing her appearance would excite comment. She contemplated running into the bedroom to avoid Eliza's gaze, but then she saw that there was no need. Her cousin had not looked at her. Refusing Cass's offer of a chair, Eliza stood gazing into the fire, rubbing her hands.

"Eliza, has something happened?" enquired Cass in her calm way.

Eliza, still lost in thought, did not speak for a moment. But then she reached for the armchair beside the fire, where she cast herself down in an attitude of studied, rather than natural, repose. Jenny placed herself in the darkest corner of the room, where Eliza would scarcely be able to make out her face even if she tried.

"Your brother James," said Eliza at last, "not half an hour ago, approached me as I sat in the drawing-room – with extremely cold fingers – and asked me to become his wife."

There was an astonished silence, during which she continued. "When I refused, which I hope you will agree I had no choice about, he picked up his hat and left the house without a word. Do not expect to see him again at Steventon while I remain here. He is too embarrassed to face me, poor man."

Throughout this speech Eliza had contemplated the view of the starry sky between the open curtains. But now she turned, and Jenny saw strain in her eyes. "Did I do right?" she asked Cass, who had sat down in the other armchair. "I seemed to have no choice, but he looked so crestfallen."

"Of course you had no choice," Cassandra assured her. "Surely you do not see yourself as the mistress of Deane Parsonage, scuttling around after Anna and dealing with parishioners?"

"Do you think so?" asked Eliza eagerly. "Truthfully? What do *you* think, Jenny?"

Jenny was aware that hearing about this latest drama of Eliza's was making her feel less wretched about her own misfortune. Nothing could not make her forget it, but it had been placed in perspective. How awkward to receive a proposal you did not want, and, having refused the man, know that for ever afterwards he would carry your rejection in his heart! Whatever ignominies women had to suffer, at least refusal was not one of them.

"A sacking apron, such as Anne used to wear to pick the fruit for preserves," she told Eliza, "would not sit well upon your silk dresses. And you could not make the preserves anyway."

Eliza's wan expression softened. "My dears, I knew you would make me feel better. It is not James himself I recoil from. It is, as you rightly say, the life of a clergyman's wife. I am too spoilt and fond of parties. I believe I told him as much. I believe I told him I could not make him happy, and that I considered us unsuited. But I cannot remember *what* I said to him. I so hope I did not hurt his feelings unduly."

"I am sure you did not," said Cassandra. "And James, you know, is such a busy, practical man, he will not settle for the life of a solitary widower. If he has failed with you, he will succeed with another woman in due course, you may be certain."

Eliza sighed. "I seem fated to disappoint," she said, turning again to the view of the sky. "I must tell you, cousins, that this is the *second* proposal of marriage I have rejected since Jean died. Am I becoming the stuff of comedy, do you think? A rich widow who sifts her suitors too well, and ends up glad to catch at the old writing-master's son?"

Jenny's heart had begun to thud at the memory of Henry hurrying along the pavement outside Eliza's house. She drew up a chair. "Eliza … if you do not mind, will you tell me when this other proposal took place?"

"Last spring," replied Eliza. "Shortly before poor Anne died, when you were staying with me at Orchard Street. Oh, what an eventful time that was!"

Cassandra, seeing Jenny's agitation, was the one to press their cousin to tell more.

"I have no objection to your knowing," said Eliza, for whom the confession was evidently something of a relief, "because I know my words will not go further than these walls. Especially, they must not come to your mama or Henry."

"Definitely not," smiled Cassandra. "He is a worse gossip than any woman!"

For the first time in her life, Jenny saw Eliza blush violently. This was astonishing enough, but Eliza went on to say, "That is not the reason that I do not wish you to speak of this to him."

After a moment's pause Cassandra spoke, with incredulity. "Do you mean that you received a proposal from *Henry*?"

Eliza nodded, still looking out of the window, still very red. "When you were staying at Godmersham he rode up to town on the pretext of some sort of errand, I believe."

"I remember!" interjected Jenny. "He went to have his hair cut."

"Oh, I blush to think of it!" confessed Eliza. "He sent me a note, and called before he rode back to Kent. He was with me only for fifteen minutes or so, but in that time he made a very affecting declaration. I must own I was tempted."

The memory of this scene had touched her. Her hands went to her blazing cheeks; her head dropped.

"What did you say to him?" asked Jenny. "And what did he say to *you*?"

"Shush, Jenny," admonished Cassandra gently. "We cannot presume to ask what passes in a private conversation of such importance."

"I do not remember my words anyway," said Eliza, looking up, "any more than I remember my words to James. I suppose I must have said that it was too soon after Jean's death. It was afterwards, when he had gone, that I walked round and round the music-room for over an hour, tormented by the expression of his eyes when he heard my refusal." She leaned forward in her chair, her beautiful face full of tenderness. "Henry, you see, though he has much to recommend him as a husband, is ten years my junior, and should have the chance to father children. But I am unwilling to risk bearing another child with the same condition as my poor Hastings. I did not say this to your brother, but he must know it all the same."

Again she broke off, closing her eyes and shaking her head as if to dispel unwelcome thoughts.

"Perhaps," offered Jenny by way of comfort, "so many reasons *not* to marry him came into your mind, you did not think carefully enough about the reasons *for* marrying him. Perhaps he will conclude this himself, and try again."

"I do not know if I wish him to," replied Eliza. "I do not know what to think."

She was silent for a moment. Then, with her complexion restored to its usual shade and the beginning of a smile on her lips, she put up her hands to tidy the back of her hair. Jenny had seen her do this before, in the company of gentlemen.

"At any rate," she said, "the poor boy must have had a very melancholy ride that evening. And I was so agitated, I slept not a wink, and must have looked wretched at my party the next day."

"You did not," Jenny assured her. "Cass and I were there."

"And of course, Henry was *not* there!" cried Cassandra, remembering. "The day before the party he rushed off to Dover for no reason, assuring us he would come to the party later. But he never did, and he never had any intention of doing so!"

Jenny's heart increased its exertions. She, and she alone, knew that Henry *had* come to Eliza's house that night. Had she maligned him, in assuming his intentions were concerned with finance, when in fact they were concerned with *romance*? Poor Henry, he must have been anxious to see Eliza alone, perhaps to press his suit further, or to offer to make amends for presuming on her affections. But everyone was still up, and instead of enjoying a private conference with Eliza, Henry would be obliged to play the part of the apologetic latecomer, indulged by his sisters, his cousin and the late-staying guests, and possibly even offered a supper of left-overs. Realizing this, his nerve had failed him. But thanks to Jenny's silence, no one would ever know that he had been in London at all.

"Do you blame him?" asked Jenny, "after his disappointment?"

"And that very evening, when Henry was sulking in Dover, Anne died," said Cassandra solemnly. "Which brings us back to the subject which began this conversation. Now that Eliza has refused the position of stepmother to little Anna, who will take it instead?"

"I cannot imagine," said Jenny. She looked at Eliza. "Are you quite sure you wish to thrust James back into the rough-and-tumble of courtship?"

"Oh, my dear, do not jest! But you know, I think he will not have much trouble. He is a very presentable man, and Deane Parsonage is quite a large house to be mistress of. Do you remember, girls, taking tea in the garden when the Lloyds lived there, when I had just heard the news about Jean? I am sure there must be a woman somewhere, who looks well in a sacking apron, Jenny, and who will be very pleased to take James for her husband."

Cassandra

The church at Ibthorpe did not look its best in January. It was too late for the surrounding elms to show their autumn colour, and too early for the crocuses lining the path to bloom. But willing gardeners had redoubled their efforts when they heard that the Reverend James Austen of Deane Parsonage was to be married in their church, to their own Mary Lloyd.

The gravel path was weeded and swept, the yews trimmed, the gravestones tidied. But the work went unseen, for on the morning of the wedding a thick covering of snow fell. The air was crisp, however, and the sun shone on the small party of Austens and Lloyds that followed the couple out of the portal. Anna, in her best bonnet and cloak, was carried in the arms of her grandmother. Her solemn face peeped out upon the world as if to say, "What is happening? Cannot I stay with my aunts and grandmama as usual, while Papa goes home to Deane with this lady? How can *she* be my mama?"

Jenny held Anna's hand, and thought for the thousandth time how lucky she herself was that both her parents had lived to see her twenty-first birthday. She resolved to visit Anna often at Deane, and have her at Steventon whenever she could. There was a brightness in the child she warmed to. At not quite four years old, Anna was already talkative and interested in everything around her, especially the stories Aunt Jane invented for her. As Anna grew up, Jenny was sure they would pass many happy hours together in the upstairs sitting-room. And when Cassandra was married she would bring her children from Shropshire, and Jenny could teach them their letters.

"How do you think the bride looks?" said Martha in Jenny's ear.

Mary, clutching her new husband's arm, was smilingly accepting congratulations. The only concession she had made to wedding finery was a small veil over her bonnet, and new gloves. But in her ordinary features Jenny saw a thawing of tension, and a hint of what could only be described as relief. For Mary, the plainer of the Lloyd sisters, living without a fortune in a country parish, marriage to a well-respected clergyman spelled the end of anxiety over her own and her family's future.

"I think the simplicity of her attire becomes her," replied Jenny. "And she looks truly happy, do you not think? As well she might."

"It is a good match for James, too," said Cassandra, who had joined them. "I welcome Mary to the family. And it means that you, Martha, are a relation. Now your sister is our sister too, you have no reason not to be at Steventon as often as distance allows."

"Dear Cass," said Martha. "I long to be inspecting *your* appearance outside a church."

"Tom hopes to return in May," said Cass.

"But it is only January!"

"Five months is a short time, Martha, compared to the five years we have waited already."

Henry approached. "Come, ladies," he said, removing his top hat with a flourish and bowing unnecessarily low. He was evidently enjoying playing the part of groomsman. "The carriages and the wedding breakfast await. Miss Martha, may I offer you my arm?"

"What if Henry were to marry Martha?" whispered Cass to Jenny as they followed.

"No, never!" replied Jenny, laughing. "Do not wish him and his monkey tricks on her!"

First Impressions was moving on apace. Of all the stories Jenny had written, it was the one whose plot fell into place most easily. Charles Bingley and the eldest Miss Bennet would overcome the obstacles placed in their way by the haughty Fitzwilliam Darcy, who would turn out to be a secret hero and marry the heroine, the irrepressible Elizabeth Bennet. And it would begin with a public ball, just like the ones she and Cass had attended at the Basingstoke Assembly Rooms, where Elizabeth and Darcy would form their "first impressions" of one another.

Now that Anna had gone back to live at Deane with her father and Mary, her Aunt Jane had more peace to write. And now that Aunt Jane was twenty-one, she considered that she looked upon the world with a more sagacious eye. She had succeeded at last in her quest to be called Jane, not by pleading or threatening, but simply by commandeering the help of her sister.

"If *you* do not call me Jenny, no one will," she had reasoned.

"Are you sure?"

"Wait and see."

James already insisted that Anna call Jenny "Aunt Jane", and had ceased to use "Jenny" himself. Under his influence so did his new wife. And because Mary did not use it, Martha and Mrs Lloyd did not use it either. It took Cassandra a while to adjust to the change, but before February was out everyone in the household seemed to have forgotten that anyone called Jenny had ever existed in their midst. In her heart, Jane knew they approved of her more grown-up appellation. Why had it taken so long to establish?

Being twenty-one *did* feel different, just as she had imagined it would. Now she could go without Cass or Mama to Godmersham and London, though, like any lady, she must have a male escort, even if the only one available was a manservant. Now she could be privy to discussions which would hitherto have been deemed unsuitable for her ears. And with the knife-mark Tom Lefroy had made in her heart still smarting, she had come of age in more than merely years.

Around her, life went on. The new term began, bringing to the Rectory two new boys, as well as the old ones, and Mama was preoccupied with the familiar task of ministering to the homesick feelings of these two tender twelve-year-olds. Letters were written to mothers, encouraging parcels from home. Toasting cheese at the drawing-room fire was allowed on Saturday evenings, as were ghost stories. Drawn especially to the more serious of the two, a boy called Edmund, Jane taught him to play piquet, the most complicated card game she knew, which Tom and Charles Fowle had taught her when *they* had been Papa's pupils.

The war with France had spread throughout Europe.

While Bonaparte's power grew on land, mutinous sailors were fuelling the relentless anxiety endured by the officers of the British navy. Frank reported that he had been obliged to have some of his men flogged. "Baby" Charles's letters were staunchly cheerful, but Mama's chin still quivered when she read them.

And the bloodshed in France went on. Jean Capot de Feuillide was now one of many, many thousands who had perished. Robespierre, this "madman" as Papa called him, was not interested in the ideals of the Revolution. He wished only to save his own skin, inflicting upon others the same ruthless tyranny for which the King and Queen of France had been murdered. Jane's heart still folded with pity whenever the memory of Eliza's husband's terrible death arose; she could not forgive his killers, however horrifying their own fate might now be.

She busied herself with domestic concerns, helping Mrs Travers with the preserving, sewing boys' shirts. The sun shone on the Rectory garden as brightly as usual, despite the dispiriting news from across the Channel, and Jane wandered about its paths and bowers with undiminished pleasure. This would probably be the last year she would have Cassandra at home, with Tom expected to return before the summer. Knowing this, Papa presented Cass with the money for her wedding dress, and Jane accompanied her to Basingstoke to buy the material.

James seemed happy enough with Mary, but after his disappointment in his first choice Jane wondered when, if ever, they would see Eliza at Steventon again. No doubt she would remarry and perhaps go to live far away, and the attentions of the Austen brothers would become as misty in her memory as the scenes from their childhood plays.

As the spring days lengthened, Jane sat on the embroidered cushion and wrote. She decided to call the eldest Miss Bennet *Jane*, in homage to her own newly acquired proper name. She wrote her own loss of Tom Lefroy into Jane's grief at the loss of Mr Bingley. But the ink flowed most freely when she created her questioning, thoughtful, loving, impulsive, merry-hearted heroine, Elizabeth Bennet.

One windy April morning, when the countryside was bright with blossom, Jane accosted her sister in the hall as she was putting on her bonnet and cloak, and read aloud a newly completed conversation between Elizabeth and Jane. "Do you like her?" she asked eagerly. "Or is she too impertinent?"

"She has exactly the right amount of impertinence to enslave Darcy," replied Cassandra.

"And you are confident she does not remind you of anyone else?"

Cass was immediately alert to the anxiety in Jane's voice. "Anyone else? What do you mean?"

"I have written of two sisters again!" wailed Jane. "The elder one is beautiful and kind and calm, like Elinor, and the younger one is impatient and unyielding and hasty, like Marianne. And Marianne was eighteen when *I* was eighteen, while Elizabeth is twenty because *I* was twenty when I began to write about her!"

"All this is perfectly understandable," said Cassandra.

"But is it not rather … limited?"

Cass gave her sister the look that meant she was about to say something quite incontrovertible. "No, Jane, it is not."

"But my novels are not like other people's," insisted Jane,

walking restlessly around the hallway. "Other novels are about haunted castles, or are stories of high romance, or are satirical like those of Samuel Richardson, whose writing I admire so greatly, Cass. The people in them have adventures that make one alternately laugh and cry. But I sometimes feel as if…" She thought for a moment, unsure how to go on. Cass waited. Then Jane continued. "I feel as if I am working on a little bit of ivory, two inches square, like a painter of miniatures."

"And do you not think the beholders of miniatures have the wit to appreciate the detail?" asked Cassandra, tying her ribbons, then, dissatisfied with the bow, untying them again.

Jane hugged the banister post, contemplating her sister with agitation. "I do not know what to think. Help me, Cass. You are wise."

"Very well. First, if you do not consider your novels satirical, then you are not reading the same words as I am. Second, readers are as satisfied with detailed portraits as with any adventures or romances. And third, you must not worry that your families of sisters are *limited*. They are *wonderfully* interesting."

"Are they?"

"Yes, they are." Cassandra checked her appearance in the hall mirror. "And you know, perfectly believable though they are, neither characters nor events bear any great resemblance to our own life here at Steventon. I do not recall a man of Darcy's wealth or Willoughby's beauty, or treachery, ever being seen in these parts, and I have not to my knowledge been cast into despair by a Mr Ferrars or a Mr Bingley, older sister though I may be."

"You are right," said Jane gratefully. "You are quite right. I may *start* with what I know, but I *finish* with fiction."

"Exactly," soothed Cassandra. "And now, will you come

to the post office with me? I am hoping for a letter from Tom, and shall only be able to bear the disappointment at not finding one if you are there."

Jane ran for her cloak, and the sisters set off along the lane as they had many times before. Jane chattered and Cassandra listened, and they admired the budding foliage as they passed, and held down their skirts against gusts of wind, laughing.

There *was* a letter from St Domingo. Cassandra descended upon it as if she would devour it. But outside the post office she caught Jane's arm. "This is not addressed in Tom's hand," she said in dismay. She turned the letter over. "Why should his commanding officer write to me?"

The sisters looked at each other. Jane saw the light go out of Cass's eyes. "Oh Jenny!" she whispered, reverting in her agitation to the old name. "I cannot… "

Fearing Cass would faint, Jane helped her to an oak seat covered with carved initials, which had stood outside the post office at Steventon for as long as they had lived there. They had played upon it with the village children, though Jane had always baulked at carving her own initials, bravely disbelieving the big boy who had told her that it would bring a curse on whoever sat there if she did not.

Cassandra did not faint. She opened the letter and began to read it, frowning her small frown. All the colour vanished from her face. Jane waited in silence.

"He is not coming back," said Cassandra faintly.

"Oh, no! Has his departure been postponed?"

"No." Cassandra's trembling fingers folded the letter, smoothed it and laid it on her lap. "He died of the cholera two months ago. We shall never see him again."

* * *

It was madness even to consider such a thing, but for a long time after that day, Jane wondered about the curse on the oaken seat. Had the village boy been right? Had *she*, by her refusal to mark the wood with her initials, brought this calamity upon her beloved sister?

She told herself that every village had a wooden seat; every village had its own nonsensical beliefs; every village had a large boy who wielded power over little girls. But then her conviction that God could not forsake so devout a servant as Cassandra would descend again. And if Tom's death was not God's will, whose was it?

Though spring continued its transformation of the landscape outside the Rectory, the days inside the house were dark. Cassandra wept and prayed by turns. Papa was so dejected that it was twenty-four hours before he summoned the will to write a letter of condolence to the Reverend and Mrs Fowle. Mama, tormented as much by her daughter's loss of prospects as by her own heartfelt grief, kept to her room.

None of the brothers were at home, and the schoolboys, as subdued by the death of "Miss Cassandra's" fiancé as if she had been their own sister, went about their business on tiptoe and forwent their garden games. For them, Jane suspected, it was an unwelcome reminder that the safe surroundings of the Reverend Austen's school, which Tom and his brother had once enjoyed, were temporary. They, like Tom, would soon face the dangers of the world. Meanwhile James, who had so recently experienced a sudden bereavement himself, visited daily with a new passage marked in his Bible, in the hope that the simple words of faith would comfort his sister.

Jane was familiar with the helplessness of bystanders at a

tragedy. She had felt it keenly when Jean Capot de Feuillide had died, alone and so far from his loved ones. When Anne had passed from life to death as swiftly as the guillotine blade travels, by her own fireside in the presence of her husband, Jane's sense of superfluity had increased. But upon the death of Tom, her helplessness took on a life of its own. It filled the room where Cassandra lay. It spread to the sitting-room, where Jane had so recently written exchanges between those two most attractive of characters, Elizabeth Bennet and Mr Darcy. She remembered how she had read them aloud to her sister, and been rewarded with Cassandra's intelligent appreciation. "They *must* marry!" she had exclaimed. "How could they ever be satisfied with anyone else?"

First Impressions had now joined *Elinor and Marianne* in the bottom of a box in the wardrobe. Jane had set her winter boots upon the lid, partly to disguise the existence of the box, partly as a gesture of finality. How could she indulge herself by making up stories about non-existent people, however witty, beautiful, clever, long-suffering and heroic, when her dear sister's world – the *real* world – had collapsed so irrevocably? Writing fiction was the pastime of a trivial nature, a mere childish game. The death of her sister's hopes would be the death of childhood. From now on she would be an adult and face life as it should be faced, with the stoicism she had seen from Eliza and James in their bereavements, and would soon see from Cassandra in hers.

For three days Jane sat at the window of the sitting-room, pretending to work or read, and thinking, thinking…

Cassandra lay on the bed in the next room, with the connecting door open so that she could alert Jane if she needed her. She ate almost nothing, barring Kitty from the room and allowing only Jane to bring her soup. After two or three mouthfuls she would lay down the spoon and gesture for her to take the bowl away. At night, she slept so fitfully that Jane offered to spend the nights in the sitting-room, in the hope of giving her more repose. But Cassandra had clung to her and begged her not to leave.

On the fourth day Jane awoke before her sister. It was early; the silvery light of a May morning crept around the curtains and the birds were in full song. Jane swallowed the lump which rose in her throat every morning when she remembered that Tom would never see another dawn. She slid out of bed and put on her house-robe as quietly as she could; but before she had found her slippers she heard Cassandra's voice.

"Are you there, Jane?"

Jane's heart swelled with compassion for the tear-streaked face on the pillow, and the small hand reaching for hers. "Would you like some breakfast?" she asked, without much hope of success.

Cassandra let go of Jane's hand and propped herself up on her elbows. "Would you open the curtains, please?" She squinted at the light as it poured in. Then she sat up and raised her arms towards the window, her expression calm. "I think I *would* like breakfast, dearest. Would you bring it yourself?"

"Do you feel different this morning?" asked Jane. Unsure how to put a question she did not truly understand the meaning of, she hesitated, and tried again. "Has something changed?"

"Something has *passed*," said Cassandra simply. "Tom is dead, and has taken my love with him to his grave. But this morning I know I shall not die; I shall go on in this world, secure in the knowledge that he loves me and is waiting for me to join him in the next world. When I do, however many years hence, we shall rejoice because we shall be together at last."

Cassandra's eyes shone with love, though for Tom or for God, Jane could not tell. A terrible peace had descended upon her sister, terrible because, at that moment, Jane knew Cassandra would never give herself to another man. She was Tom's widow, though they had never been married, and she would remain his faithful companion for the rest of her days.

Jane embraced her. Neither spoke for a long time. Jane fought against the memory of the letter-burning, when it had been she herself in need of comfort. Cassandra's loss was so much worse; how could she, Jane, be so self-centered as to make any comparison? Yet the memory *did* rise, and lay in Jane's breast until Cassandra broke the embrace.

To Jane's unutterable relief, the smile she had thought never to see again glimmered in her sister's eyes. "Breakfast?" she reminded her. "I would like to eat it at the work-table, like we always used to. Will you fetch my robe for me? We can get dressed later."

Jane fingered Cassandra's mourning gown, which lay, neatly folded, on the lid of the chest at the foot of the bed. "How long do you intend to wear black, Cass? If Tom had been your husband, it would be a year. But is there another rule for a fiancé?"

"I shall order several more black gowns," said Cassandra, beginning to undo her braid. "I shall never wear colours again."

Jane was shocked into saying the sort of thing that she would have despised, had it come from the lips of Madam

Lefroy or Mrs Bigg. "But what will people say?"

"I care not what people say," returned Cass. "*You* may have as many white and printed gowns as you wish, Jane, and go into society whenever the opportunity presents itself. But I shall not, and that is the end of it."

Jane knew better than to protest further. Unwilling to distress her sister, she went to get the breakfast. But as she climbed the stairs with the tray she felt convinced that her sister's avowal of lifelong mourning was extreme. Eliza was back in her social round, rejecting present suitors and wearing gifts from previous ones. James was married again, less than two years after Anne had died. Jane did not expect *this* of her sister – she understood the profundity of feeling which had made Cassandra turn her face against marriage – but it was tragic for a lovely young woman to resign herself to black clothes for ever.

Self-centered though it might be, Jane feared for her own future. If Cass would not go with her into society, who would? And even if she could persuade her sister to do so, what would be a stranger's perception of these two young women, the younger prettily dressed and on the look-out for partners, the elder in black and refusing to dance? Would Jane ever enjoy a ball again? By the time she set the tray down on the work-table she was convinced that a life of no writing *and* no parties stretched before her to the grave.

Cassandra ate with more relish than Jane herself could muster. Seeing that her sister was unwilling to speak, Cass tried to draw her on an irresistible subject. "What has the delightful Elizabeth Bennet been doing lately?"

"Nothing."

"Why not? Is she ill?"

"No, she is deplorably healthy for a character in a book," said Jane. "Her mama will never have any scares about her, not that Mrs Bennet would care anyway, as her favourite is the youngest sister, Lydia. But I have not written any more of *First Impressions* since ... we received the news."

"Then you must start again immediately."

"I am never going to write any more of that or any other book," said Jane, looking down at her hands, which were clasped uncomfortably in her lap. She had no wish to witness her sister's bewilderment.

But Cass was not bewildered. Her tone was as near to vexed as Jane had ever heard it. "Have you made this resolution because of *my* resolution, about the mourning clothes?" she demanded strictly, as if she were testing a Sunday-school child.

"Of course not," Jane protested, looking up. "I hid the manuscript on the day we heard the news, and decided never to look at it again. In a world where a young man can die so pointlessly I feel a fool to be making up stories."

"A fool? A *fool*?" repeated Cassandra. "I *insist* that you take out the manuscript and put it back on the desk where it belongs!" She waved her bread and butter about in her agitation. "You are not a fool, Jane, you are a writer of rare gifts, who is capable of giving great joy. And it is precisely *because* things like Tom's death happen that the world *needs* literature. It needs art, and music, and plays."

Jane shook her head, unsure whether to be flattered by or contemptuous of her sister's words. "But novels are frivolous, are they not?"

"God would not see them as frivolous. He has given you this gift and He does not expect His bounty to go unused. You must finish this book and send it to a publisher, and show the world your talent. Do you not see? My disappointment in love *must not* be yours in literature."

As Cassandra said this the tension which had racked Jane's limbs relented. She untangled her hands. An idea had occurred to her.

"All right, Cass, let us strike a bargain. If I go on with *First Impressions*, might you be persuaded out of mourning in, say … a year?"

Cassandra's expression hovered on the edge of dismay. But then her shoulders eased themselves. Her neck lengthened, her chin tilted, and she suddenly looked to Jane like the Cassandra she had always known, a beloved inspiration for her own attempts to acquire beauty, grace and good humour. "You sly thing!" she cried. "You see, you will always outwit everyone, just like Elizabeth Bennet!"

Then she dropped the remains of her bread and butter, put her hands over her face and began to sob so bone-shakingly that Jane was unable to soothe her. Despairingly, as Mama's night-capped head and worried expression appeared round the door, Jane wondered if, despite her sister's brave words, Cassandra's heart was not broken beyond repair.

BOOK THREE

Betrayed

Papa

*T*he marriage register at Steventon Church was a heavy book in leather covers. It lay open at the present date of 1797 on its sloping table in the registry, with a thick silk ribbon marking the place. Each entry was written neatly, followed by the man's and woman's signatures, or, in the case of illiterate parishioners, a cross.

Jane had lingered after the service. She stood before the altar, observing how the morning sunshine brightened the east window and splashed its splendour on the stones beneath her feet. *Tom*, she thought, *Thomas Lefroy, if you are in church this morning, are you thinking of me, or only of your prayers?*

Quickly, she went into the registry and laid aside the ribbon. She turned the register's pages until she found the place she sought. It was still there, then. Papa had not torn it out, as he had threatened.

Jenny's eyes filled with tears. Years ago, when she was sixteen, she had turned to a blank page near the back of the register and written in her own imaginary marriage entry. It had been a little girl's game. Her father had laughed when he saw it, especially since she had experimented with several different husbands.

She looked at the husbands' names. With a stab she noticed that one of them, a Mr Fitzwilliam, was the name she had used for Mr Darcy's first name in *First Impressions*. How strange that this fictitious Fitzwilliam was so potent in her imagination that he had appeared, then been forgotten, then appeared again.

Her tears dried; interest had overcome them. She ran her finger down the other made-up names. They were evidently supposed to be gentlemen, of varying grandeur, some with three or even four names. They came from all over England, from London to the north country and back again. None from Ireland, she noted. Then, right at the bottom of the page, when she had perhaps been tiring of the game, she had written a simple name, like that of a farm labourer, next to her own. *That is what made Papa laugh*, she told herself. *What a nonsensical girl I was!*

She did not close the book, nor did she find the current page again. She stood there, in her bonnet and gloves, and the black silk jacket which had once belonged to Anne and did not fit Mary, thinking, thinking...

Did Tom Lefroy remember that on their very first meeting he had asked her to call him Tom, and called her Jane? She had never met a gentleman who had shown anything approaching such intimacy with her. For over a year now she had nursed the memory of those three meetings: the first at that Christmas ball, the second the next day, when he had visited the Rectory with George Lefroy. She could still see Tom, nervously clutching his hat, asking her for the first dance at the forthcoming ball at his aunt and uncle's house, the scene of that third and final encounter.

She could still feel Mama's pearls around her neck, and hear the rustle of the hem of Cassandra's pink dress. She saw Tom's ravishing smile, which bore out what she had heard about the charm of the Irish, since his father had something of it too. She felt the pressure of his hand through her glove when he had led her to the floor for the last dance, and recalled everyone in the room looking at them. The room itself – every candelabra, every garland of winter greenery, the position of every musician, every footman – was fixed timelessly in her memory.

Had he forgotten it all? Or did he, like Jane, permit himself the occasional fantasy that opposition to their match would somehow fall away, and he would send the tenderest letter ever written by a man to a woman, hoping that her affections remained as warm as his? Of course, she would reply that they did, and within days he would arrive at Steventon, not quite on a white horse, but in a carriage, and march straight into the study to speak to Papa.

Jane turned back to 1797 and put the ribbon in place. The fantasy was as impossible as the dreams of the sixteen-year-old and her Mr Fitzwilliam. Without a backward glance she walked out of the registry, along the aisle and out of the door. In the churchyard she put up her parasol against the midday glare. It threw a black shadow, and, since the Rectory garden was no more than a few steps away, she was glad to hide her face.

Martha Lloyd had come over from Ibthorpe for a week's stay with her sister at Deane Parsonage. The day after her arrival

Jane and Cass took the lane to Deane, a walk more familiar than any other, to visit their friend. Seated upon a hard chair at the parlour fireside with Martha, Cass and Mary, Jane almost felt as if recent trying events had never occurred, and the four of them were carefree girls again. Martha, eager to hear about Jane's latest work, had absorbed the plot of *First Impressions* with her usual keenness, and was now ready to question it.

"Would *you* accept a man whom you had refused before?" she asked Jane. "If someone insulted *me* as deeply as Mr Darcy insults Elizabeth, I should never speak to him again."

"But Elizabeth is prejudiced against Darcy long before that," put in Cassandra loyally. "And after her conclusions are proved too hasty, she realizes that she wants to marry him after all."

"And he is rich, and handsome," added Mary with a smile.

"I still think she would not do it," insisted Martha, "though I am prepared to wager, ladies, that our clever Jane will write it in such a way as to make it the most natural thing in the world."

"May I speak?" asked Jane meekly. "As Elizabeth's creator, I feel my knowledge of her to be somewhat more profound than anyone else's."

"There you are, Martha!" cried Mary. "That is politeness itself, but of course it really means, 'Martha Lloyd, you do not know what you are talking about'."

"Not at all," Jane assured Martha. "All observations are useful. And I confess, I am unsure whether I *can* make the second proposal convincing. What must Darcy say that will excuse his former conduct, capture Elizabeth *and* satisfy the reader?"

"Oh, that is easy!" cried Martha. "I suggest that he says, 'Miss Bennet, my passion for you has made me as noble in character as I am in rank, and if you do not marry me I shall quit Pemberley for ever and live as a beggar on Cheapside.'"

During the ensuing laughter Mary stood up and smoothed her skirt. "Jane, dear, I wish you the very best with your story, but writing it appears very complicated. I am very glad I am only the mistress of a parsonage, and do not have to consider such things. Now, shall I bring tea? Or wine? And some cake?"

When she had gone Martha reached across and patted Jane's hand. "The book is going to be wonderful. What shall become of it when it is finished?"

Jane kicked the edge of the hearthrug gently. "It will join its predecessors in a box, I predict."

"No, it will not!" protested Cassandra. "This one *must* be sent to a publisher, I insist."

"Have your parents read any of it?" enquired Martha.

"Yes," Jane told her, glancing at Cassandra. "Perhaps, when it is completed, Papa may decide if it is good enough. Will that satisfy you, Cass? I shall do nothing without his permission."

"Very well," returned Cassandra. "But he will give it willingly. He is so proud of you."

"He is a representative of the Church, however, and some of the clergy consider novels immoral, or at best unscholarly."

"You are a very good daughter," said Martha with approval. "I confess if I had written a novel I would be so pleased with myself such scruples would not deter me from publication." Her eyes brightened. "If you did publish *First Impressions*, Jane, would it bear your real name?"

"I have not considered the question," said Jane uncertainly.

"Perhaps to confound disapproving clergymen, you could pretend to be a man," suggested Martha with glee. "Mr

Janus Austentatious!"

Jane laughed, but her heart was heavy. She knew that *First Impressions* had promise, and some scenes were undoubtedly among the best things she had ever written. When she had read the opening chapter to Henry, he had protested that Mr and Mrs Bennet were so comic they should have a whole book of their own, or better still, a play. But good though the book was, Jane was convinced it was not yet good enough for a public airing, and perhaps never would be.

She resolved to review it that very evening. If Papa were to approve of it, it must be light, and bright, and sparkling, but enforce the moral described by the title: first impressions are not always the correct ones. Elizabeth and her sisters must be exuberant, but over-exuberance must be punished, and virtue rewarded. And what if Martha's misgivings were correct, and nobody would believe that Mr Darcy would risk a second proposal to Elizabeth after she had refused him so vehemently? What could she do to *make* them believe it?

On the walk home, she was silent.

"If I were Catherine Bigg, I would say 'A penny for your thoughts, Miss Jane?'" said Cassandra eventually.

"Thank goodness you are not," replied Jane. "It is to you, not Catherine, that I will admit freely my concern about the ending of *First Impressions*. I do not wish a lapse in credibility to spoil the story."

"It is only Martha's opinion that there *is* a lapse," said Cass. "She may be wrong."

"No, she is right," insisted Jane. "And I am grateful to her for pointing it out. But what can I do?"

"Do nothing," advised Cassandra as they came within sight of the Rectory. She waved to Mama, who was waiting for Dick to bring the trap round. "Something will suggest itself to you when you least expect it. Where do you think Mama is going?"

She did not have to ask. "Girls, I am going to call upon Madam Lefroy," called their mother. "Do you have any message I can take to her?"

"Only our love, as usual," returned Cassandra.

"Mama might ask her if she has any opinions upon the endings of novels," added Jane, aside to her sister, "since she has an opinion upon everything else."

"Observe, my dear," Papa said to Mama as they and their daughters entered the Rectory one winter evening after a visit to the Biggs. "I believe this is Henry's hand."

Picking up a letter from the hall table, he showed it to his wife.

"Indeed it is," she confirmed, busy with her cloak-strings.

Cass went to her father's side. "Open it quickly, Papa. Henry almost never writes."

"Exactly," said Papa. "The occasion must be momentous. Or perhaps he wants to borrow money."

"Let us go into the drawing-room to hear it, whatever it is," suggested Mama. "My feet are ready to drop off from cold."

The candles had not been lit in the drawing-room. Kitty was with her mother in the village, as always on a Saturday night, and Travers was probably asleep by the kitchen fire. Dick would have been found in the tavern at Deane, if anyone had cared to look for him. The fire threw across the room the mobile half-light that was one of Jane's favourite wintertime sights.

The room seemed smaller than usual, with its farther reaches in darkness. The family sat down in a circle around the hearth, Jane seizing the opportunity to take her childhood place on the footstool. Papa, adjusting his spectacles, held the opened letter before the glowing logs and read the first words.

"My goodness!" he exclaimed. "Henry is to be married!"

Mama let out a small shriek. "*Not* that red-haired baggage who has been following him about for the last six months? George, tell me immediately who is to be my next daughter-in-law!"

Papa's face, lit by the full blaze of the fire, was full of astonishment and relief. "My dear, he is to marry Eliza!"

"*Eliza?*" repeated Mama, astonished. "Do you mean *our* Eliza?"

Cassandra was sitting in the chair nearest to Jane's footstool. Her hand crept out from under her skirt, where she had been keeping it warm, and rested upon Jane's shoulder. Jane looked at her. She was smiling joyfully.

"I do indeed," said Papa, consulting the letter. His surprise had quickly given way to smiling approval. "They are to be married in London next month. It is all settled."

"But Henry is ten years younger than she is!" protested Mama.

"If he were ten years *older* than his bride, Mama, you would not even mention it," interjected Jane.

"Do not be impertinent," said Mama. She looked suspiciously from Jane to Cassandra. "Has Henry ever spoken to either of you of his intention to court Eliza?"

"No," answered Jane truthfully. It was, after all, *Eliza* who had spoken of it. "We are as surprised as you."

"But we are sure it will be a happy match," said Cassandra warmly. "Is it not delightful when two people already related, and beloved by their family, join together in marriage?"

"Indeed it is," agreed Papa, looking very satisfied. "You will accustom yourself to the news, I have no doubt," he said to Mama, rising. "I shall fetch a bottle of wine, so that we may drink the health of the engaged couple. Then we shall compose a reply, congratulating Henry on his good fortune. This is a very happy outcome, after Eliza's sufferings. The Lord has worked his wonders, you see."

When he had gone, and Mama was busily reading Henry's letter for herself, Jane pulled Cass's hand. Her sister bent down to hear her.

"Do you see?" whispered Jane gleefully. "I had nothing to be anxious about. Men *do* propose a second time, and women *do* change their minds!"

When Jane had made a fair copy of *First Impressions*, placed all the pages on top of one another and tied them up with string, she was surprised at the height of the pile.

"But when it is printed, you know," reflected Cassandra, inspecting the bundle, "it will be a normal-sized book."

"It looks like the food parcels Mama sends to Frank and Charles," said Jane doubtfully. "I cannot believe it will ever be a book, normal-sized or otherwise."

"Papa insists upon writing to a publisher about it, though," Cass reminded her, "and when Papa insists upon something it always comes to pass, as you have probably noticed."

"Indeed."

Cass, who had picked up her sewing again, glanced at her sister knowingly before she made the next stitch. "You are nervous about Papa's plan."

"I confess I am," said Jane, fingering the string around the first volume. "I want my work to be seen, and yet I fear ridicule."

"That is understandable."

"Only to you, because you always understand me. To other people it seems fanciful, even absurd. I can hear Mary, for instance, saying, 'but if you write it, Jane, surely you want people to read it. Otherwise, you have wasted your time.'"

"And Mary's opinion is the only one worth listening to, of course," said Cassandra.

Jane hung her head.

"And as for 'other people' in general," said Cass, "when they produce novels as accomplished as this one, then let them regard your reticence as absurd. Now, take your precious parcel down to Papa and rejoice in your imminent appearance among the literary lions."

Jane picked up the manuscript. "However many books I publish, I shall never, ever be a lion. I am quite content to be a literary lamb, if there is such a thing."

In the study Papa handled the tied-up papers as tenderly as if they might crumble at his touch. "I have decided, my dear," he told Jane, "to write an introductory letter to Messrs Thomas Cadell & Company, a publisher in London. I understand that is the correct way to approach this matter, rather than send the whole manuscript."

Jane tried not to show her disappointment. "When shall you send it, then?"

"When I receive a reply inviting me to do so. I am told that if one sends the work without an introductory letter, the publisher merely sends it straight back, and I do not wish to risk your novel *twice* in the post for nothing."

"Are you sure, Papa?" Jane wondered who had told her father this, and on what authority.

"Quite sure. I shall wait until Messrs Cadell request it. Then they will be much more likely to accept it for publication."

"Very well." Jane once more gathered the manuscript into her arms. "And you will inform me the instant you hear anything?"

"Of course. I shall write today. I predict we shall hear by the time a fortnight has passed."

"Thank you, Papa."

A fortnight seemed to Jane a very long time. Every day she went to the post office herself, only leaving Kitty to collect the letters when circumstances decreed. Kitty's habit was to leave the letters on a silver tray on a table just inside the front door, weighting the pile against windy weather by a small, solid glass globe Frank had brought home from one of his voyages. After her search for a letter bearing the Cadell seal, Jane would replace the paperweight and walk away, her brain already busy with the following day's collection and inspection. And a little more than a week after Papa had sent his letter, the reply from the publishers appeared on the silver tray.

Her heartbeat quickening, Jane turned the letter over and over. She knew her father would be working on his sermon, but she knocked on the study door nevertheless.

"Please read it, Papa," she begged, holding out the letter to him. "Read it now."

Papa broke the seal and read aloud, "*Sir, we thank you for your proposal but regret we must decline your offer of a manuscript for publication. We remain your humble servants, etc., etc.*"

"May I see the letter?" asked Jane. She felt hot and cold at the same time. Disappointed, yet relieved. "It was written by a clerk, was it not?"

"I fear it was," said Papa. "I am sorry, my dear. But we can try another publisher. Mr John Murray, I understand, is a competent one."

"Please do not write to him, Papa," requested Jane. "I do not mind in the least if none of my stories ever finds a publisher."

"But Jane…"

"I am in earnest," insisted Jane. "The world will be no different for the lack of *First Impressions*, you know. Thank you for trying, but it is of no consequence to me."

Upstairs, she opened the cupboard door, took her boots off the lid of the box and put *First Impressions* at the bottom, under *Elinor and Marianne*.

Foolish, foolish girl, she reprimanded herself. *Regard this blow to your vanity as a reminder that parental pride, not objective judgement, was in operation here. Do not let yourself be fooled by it again.*

Catherine

*M*arriage might be in the air, but so was its natural successor, childbirth. Everybody, it seemed to Jane, was having babies. The confinements of several Steventon women kept Mama and Cassandra busy visiting, and Jane was put to use helping to mend, sort, replace and augment the stocks of baby clothes and blankets to be lent to needy parishioners. Meanwhile James and Mary's first child was expected, and in Kent, five-year-old Fanny was soon to be presented with an addition to her collection of three younger brothers.

We pray, wrote sister-in-law Elizabeth to Cassandra, *for a sister for Fanny this time. It would make Edward and me very happy if she were to forge with her sister as close a tie as you, my dear Cass, have forged with Jane. I have long been persuaded that sisterly friendship is selfless, noble and affectionate beyond all other.*

"Selfless, noble and affectionate!" cried Jane, picking up her basket and scissors. Cass was reading her letter in the garden, where she and Jane were gathering lavender for scent-bags. "To be sure, I sometimes wonder if having all these babies is weakening Elizabeth's brain."

"Jane! I sincerely hope you do not speak so harshly of *me* when I am not in your presence. In my opinion, Elizabeth's sentiment is rather beautiful."

It was now over a year since Tom's death, and, true to her bargain with Jane, Cass had removed her deep mourning. Of her two new gowns, however, one was plain dove grey and the other a colour Jane described to herself as "fieldmouse". Her hopes of ever seeing her sister clad in white sprigged muslin, with her bright beauty framed by a straw hat trimmed with pink ribbons – always a favourite summer combination – had vanished.

"Then I take back my unkind words," said Jane lightly, "and you will forgive me, as you always do. But, you know, I greatly look forward to seeing Fanny next week. She seems to me an uncommonly intelligent child."

"She is," agreed Cass with a mild smile, "and a lucky one. Her father is rich, her mother is accomplished and well-connected, she is pretty, and she is musical. "

"And she may soon have the opportunity of experiencing *sisterly friendship!*" added Jane. "What further delights could we wish upon our niece?"

Cassandra put Elizabeth's letter in the pocket of her apron. Jane knew that her sister was watching her stoop and cut and lay the lavender sprays in the basket, but she did not return her look.

"Jane, is something amiss?" asked Cassandra. "I fear you are not well. Let us go and sit in the shade, and I shall ask Kitty to bring some cordial for you."

Jane straightened up to face Cass, but she did not put her basket down. "I am perfectly well," she said. "I merely feel…" She looked around the garden, as if it would provide the words to describe the restlessness in her heart. "I feel ... left behind, somehow."

"Left behind?" Cassandra was puzzled. "But you are to accompany us to Kent."

Jane hurried to explain. "No, not literally left behind. I mean that I want to do things." She thought for a moment. "I suppose what I want is my own Fitzwilliam Darcy, complete with blazing intelligence, strict morals, a handsome figure and a country seat, so that I can be mistress of my own house and family."

Cass did not speak. The small frown had appeared. From long experience she waited for her sister to frame her thoughts, and share them without further prompting.

"It is all these new babies, Cass, which are disturbing my peace," complained Jane. "Do you remember how excited we were when Fanny and Anna were born, and we first became aunts? But by the end of this year we shall be aunts *seven times over*, and that figure can only increase. Why, Frank and Charles are not even married yet, but when they are, we shall be aunts to yet *more* children."

"And one day you shall be mother to your own, too," said Cassandra.

"I hope so," said Jane gently. Then, after a pause, "Does it not pain you, dearest, that *you* will never have a child?"

"No," replied Cassandra decisively. She pressed her lips together, to stop herself betraying even the smallest tremble, before she spoke again. "My children were buried with Tom. I have mourned them already."

Jane could not bear to hurt her sister by voicing her deepest anxiety. Since that dreadful day when the news from the West Indies had come, had not her own prospects of marriage and motherhood materially diminished? She and Cass had each loved only one man, now torn away from them by death and distance. Cass had decided not to look for another love, and Jane, after two years without a word, had accepted that Tom Lefroy was lost to her. Was she indeed left behind, doomed to spinsterhood by association? Would she for ever be one of the Misses Austen, invited out of politeness and seated next to the Samuel Blackalls and John Lyfords of this world?

She fell back on flippancy. "Twenty-two and ready for marriage!" she cried. "Young lady for sale! Roll up, roll up! What will you wager, pretty miss, on your sister's prospects? A bright new sixpence?"

"Oh, stop that," said Cassandra, going back to her cutting. "We are going to Godmersham next week, where there are always parties. And did you know that Mama is plotting to take you to Bath? If you do not meet a suitable gentleman in that notorious marriage-market, it will be because there is not one there who deserves you."

But Jane's spirits refused to revive. "I detest Bath, and I do not want to be 'deserved'," she said frostily. "I want to be loved by a man who understands the world and is prepared to laugh at it. In fact, not like Mr Darcy at all, who never laughs at anything. Is that too much to ask?"

"No, not at all," said Cass, mystified by Jane's bitter tone. "You have every cause to be optimistic. Observe the happy ending to Eliza's search."

"Eliza and Henry?" exclaimed Jane, clapping her hand to her forehead. "What comedy! What charm! Anything can happen to anyone, and not only in novels!"

Cassandra did not smile. "I remain convinced that you need that cordial. You are overwrought."

"Perhaps I am." Jane put her basket down abruptly and gathered her skirt. "If anyone is looking for me, I shall be lying down. I feel a sick headache coming on." She turned to go into the house, then back to her sister, who stood nonplussed beside the lavender bed. "Oh, and if I should die, you may write upon my tombstone, 'Here lies one whose youthful cynicism disgusted her family, but whose pretty stories delighted them.'"

"Jane, dear… " began Cass, very concerned.

"No more, Cass. Leave me be."

Cass did not dissent. She left her sister alone, and Jane lay on the bed with her feelings too tightly strung for sleep. Refusing dinner, she slipped out of the kitchen door and cried for a quarter of an hour among the shadows of the larches at the bottom of the garden. Then she joined Mama and Cass at Friday evensong.

Papa prayed for the family's safe journey into Kent, as well for his ailing parishioners and the health of the King. Cass slid Jane a sideways glance as she took her place in the family pew, and twitched a small smile. Whether or not she understood Jane's reasons for her outburst was not certain. But she bore no ill will, and Jane was absolved.

The whole family was going to Godmersham. Mindful of her sister's words, Jane packed her white dresses with as light a heart as she could, and included her writing materials. Her mornings would be free of chores. In the afternoons there would be outings, and the evenings would be passed pleasantly in company. She would begin to write again, she was sure.

Elizabeth's swollen figure betrayed the nearness of her time. Jane kissed her with real feeling, struck by how thin her face had become. She did not resemble very closely the peach-fleshed young matron who had admired Canterbury Cathedral with them only three years before. Jane knew she should not confuse fact and fiction, but she wondered whether, once engaged in producing the heirs to the Darcy fortune, that other radiant Elizabeth would lose her sparkle so soon.

A little girl stood shyly by the door, holding tightly to her nurse's hand. Her smaller brother held the woman's other hand. Both children were dressed "for company", their eyes bright with excitement at the promise of sweets and treats which Grandpapa and Grandmama's visits always brought.

"Fanny, Edward!" cried their mother, holding out her hands. "That will be all, Susanna," she instructed the nurse-maid. "You may collect the children in half an hour."

Fanny was bolder than three-year-old Edward. At her grandmama's smiling invitation she climbed upon the sofa and settled at her side, her feet dangling some inches above the floor. She smoothed her skirt. "I have a new dress," she announced.

"So I see," said Mama. "And has your hair been curled? How grown-up you look."

"Her hair curls naturally," said Elizabeth, her arms around little Edward. "Just like her aunts'."

"I am going to be a writer, like Aunt Jane," was Fanny's next announcement.

Her father guffawed. "Then you had better make the most of Aunt Jane's visit, and find out how to do it. Though since you are still learning your letters, I predict we shall wait some time for your first manuscript."

Fanny, only half-understanding, joined in the laughter. Jane watched her fondly. What a dear child she was. She did not have Anna's thoughtful air, nor her little-womanish daintiness, but she was, as Cassandra had said, a happy child – secure in the admiration of her parents, strong-willed enough to try her nurse, but possessed of enough charm to compensate for this in the eyes of her elders. In Anna, Jane saw herself as a child; in Fanny, she saw the child she wished she had been.

"Aunt Jane shall help me with my letters," said Fanny, enjoying the attention, "and Aunt Cassandra shall help me with my needlework."

There was more laughter. "But what if Aunt Jane's stitches are smaller and neater than mine?" asked Cass playfully. "Could Aunt Cassandra not be the teacher of letters?"

"No, indeed," said Fanny gravely. "I want Aunt Jane."

"Come, Fanny," said Elizabeth, holding out her hand. "Will you and Edward show Grandpapa your wooden animals? He can tell you the names of them all."

Fanny ran to the chest where the Noah's Ark lived, pursued by the shorter legs of her brother. The company's attention diverted, Jane whispered to her sister, "So I am the lady of letters, and you are the seamstress. The bluestocking and the blind woman. I trust you are as gratified as I am?"

Hot day followed hot day. "My heart goes out to Elizabeth," remarked Cass on a particularly humid afternoon, when their sister-in-law had retired to her apartment with an ice-pack on her forehead. "Mama says she is carrying a boy, for certain, all in front and none at the sides. But to be carrying a baby of either sex, in any position, in this weather must be trying."

Boy or not, the baby's kicking would sometimes disturb the loose silk robe Elizabeth wore. This amused Edward, who joked that the baby must indeed be a boy, eager to make his way into the world before the grouse shooting season started.

Jane thought she had never seen her brother look so well. Tall like all the Austen brothers, his serene countenance spoke of a man at home in his setting, at one with the world. He had prepared a busy itinerary for his guests. They made excellent use of the barouche, calling on Edward and Elizabeth's friends, and also visited Margate and Whitstable, where little Edward was introduced to oysters. His expression upon tasting them amused everyone in the party except Fanny, who put a sisterly arm around his shoulders and scolded her papa for laughing.

Elizabeth, who did not join them on their outings, was surrounded every evening by her husband's family, fatigued but high-spirited, each competing with the others to tell her in the most amusing detail of the day's adventures. Edward sat at the head of the table, pouring wine and smiling, and Jane retired at night to her single bedroom – a luxury less welcome than Elizabeth supposed – and stared at the white page. She had written nothing since the letter from Messrs Cadell had come. Think as hard as she might, no inspiration entered her head.

Three weeks passed in this way. The plan was for Jane and her parents to return to Steventon, leaving Cass to be with Elizabeth during and after her confinement. Jane wondered what this "being with" entailed, and how long it would be before she would be asked to perform the same duty for a sister-in-law. It was another indication that Cassandra, at the age of twenty-five, was no longer considered to be a young woman with a young woman's concerns. How quickly this change had occurred, and how irrevocable it seemed.

On their last day they took breakfast on the terrace. Though ten o'clock had not yet struck, the sun beat heavily upon the iron-hard garden. The potted plants upon the parapet hung their heads; the fountain in the middle of the lawn was dry. From the shade of her parasol Jane surveyed the view of Godmersham's grounds.

She did not know when she would see them again. Journeys of greater distance than could be accomplished on foot were gifts to be given, not requested. It would not be until Jane was mistress of her own house, with her own servants and her own carriage, that she would be able to plan her own visits. She would certainly come to Godmersham, and go to see Eliza and Henry in London. But of course she would also learn to appreciate other, as yet unknown, places, associated with the man who was to provide such freedom – her husband.

She pondered on this, and him, as she fixed in her memory the white house and the green park under a bright blue sky. She longed to be at Steventon again. Even without Cass's presence, the upstairs sitting-room would be a haven of peace in a way the pretty bedroom at Godmersham could never be. She craved employment, and there would be plenty to keep her busy at home. Mary's baby was due soon; there would be more village babies, and the usual summer task of fruit and vegetable preserving. Three weeks would have made a great difference to the lettuces and cress she was growing under the kitchen window. They could not be preserved, so Mrs Travers had probably already given most of the crop to the pig. With no family at home, Jane wondered how she and Kitty and Dick had passed the time. She smiled at the prospect of watching Mama find out.

When the time came to be gone, Jane took an affectionate leave of her sister. "Kiss the new baby for me," she instructed her, "and when you come back to Hampshire you will be just in time to kiss Mary's baby too."

"Take care," said Cass, embracing Jane, "and do not neglect your correspondence. I shall look daily for a letter."

Jane longed to write something light-hearted. *First Impressions* made people laugh, but it also told of serious things. After the catastrophe that had befallen Cassandra, and her own disappointment, it would be refreshing to write a story built upon nothing but a joke.

Her new heroine, she decided, would be as ordinary as she could make her. She would not dash through the book making men fall in love with her, with a serene older sister as a foil. She would be an innocent, an enthusiastic novel-reader who was inclined to believe that the supernatural events of *The Castle of Otranto* or *The Mysteries of Udolpho* might be real. Her discovery that they were not, and her simultaneous discovery of love, would give the story the lightness of touch that Jane sought.

Upon her return from Godmersham she searched the desk drawers for *Lady Catherine,* an adventure story begun when she was sixteen. There was no doubt it was nonsense, but Jane still liked the name. Without the "Lady" it would be very suitable for her ordinary heroine. There were only a few chapters, since she never finished anything in those days. When she read them they made her laugh and cringe by turns.

She looked out of the window for a while. Then she walked round and round the room a few times. At last she picked up the pen and paper, sat down on her window-seat cushion, chewed the end of the pen for a moment, and began to make an outline.

"Jane! Ja–ane!" called Mama up the stairs. "Have you forgotten we are going to the Biggs'? Come along!"

Sighing, Jane went to the top of the stairs. Papa and Mama, who was wearing an uncomfortably new-looking, close-fitting bonnet and her best shawl, waited at the bottom. "Are you sure it is today?" asked Jane.

"Quite sure," said Mama. "And we shall be late if you do not make haste."

"I must put on my best white."

"Yes, you must. Shall I send Kitty up?"

"No, I can manage."

Jane tidied away her papers, washed her face sketchily, changed her dress and collected her summer shawl and white bonnet, gloves and parasol. Much as she liked the Biggs, she had little enthusiasm for a visit when she had something so much more pressing to attend to. In Kent there had seemed nothing to write about; in Hampshire there was suddenly a great deal, and she was impatient to begin.

Mr and Mrs Bigg were holding an "at home", an afternoon gathering of about twenty guests. Manydown, though not as grand as Godmersham, was a very pleasant house for such a event. It possessed a fine conservatory, or loggia, as Mrs Bigg preferred to call it, designed in the Italian style and decorated with growing foliage. Even Mama, with her dread of sitting near an open window, was tempted out there by the comfortable furniture, the footmen offering sweetmeats and the warmth of the air.

Everyone present was known to the Austens: John Portal, his parents and his new fiancée; the Lyfords, the Lloyds and the Lefroys. Jane noted the absence of Samuel Blackall with relief, and that of John Harwood with understanding. Elizabeth was not there; she had married William Heathcote and gone to live more than a hundred miles away. Jane had no difficulty in putting herself in John Harwood's shoes. If the Irish Lefroys were ever to invite her to a party, and Tom was not there because he had married someone else, could Jane honestly say she would go?

Martha Lloyd embraced her friend affectionately. "When are you and Cass going to come to us at Ibthorpe?" she demanded. "Mama and I are greatly in need of visitors and gossip now that Mary has gone off to be your sister-in-law."

"We shall come whenever you care to invite us," replied Jane warmly.

"And how fares my sister?"

"She is well, if a little heavier than she used to be."

Martha laughed delightedly. "I must confess to excitement at the prospect of a niece or nephew, you know."

"Martha, you will not say that when James and Mary are about to have their sixth or seventh child!"

"I suppose that is true," agreed Martha. Then, taking Jane's arm, she added, "And speaking of sisters-in-law, have you heard that Charles Fowle is engaged to be married? A Miss Townsend, according to Mrs Fowle. If Cass had married Tom, this Miss T. would have been her sister-in-law. Did Mrs Fowle write to your mother?"

"Perhaps, but no letter has arrived," said Jane a little breathlessly. A sudden thud of her heart had constricted her lungs. Charles Fowle, her childhood friend, fondly destined for her by everyone except herself, had severed those Steventon strings for ever. And in truth, however unwillingly she had endured other peoples' predictions of their union, Jane had always regarded him as available if all else failed. "So finally, Martha," she continued, "we may put that whole business to rest. Charles Fowle was never interested in marrying me, nor I in marrying him."

"And when was that ever a hindrance to a betrothal?" asked Martha with an arch look. When Jane did not respond she hurriedly fluttered her fan, looking round the room. "The heat in here is intolerable. Let us go into the garden, where there are ices, so Catherine tells me, and we can discuss the merits of matrimony in peace."

"Ices!" was all Jane managed to say before she found herself propelled out of the conservatory and across the grass to where Alethea and Catherine Bigg sat beneath an awning, dripping melted ice onto their gowns and giggling.

"Good afternoon, ladies!" trilled Alethea. "See how clever our cook is? These are delicious!"

Jane was determined not to allow Martha's news and the loss of her writing hours to inhibit her enjoyment. She sat down in the shade and accepted an ice from a footman's tray.

Martha sat back contentedly in her chair. "The Bigg family surely gives the best parties in England."

"Perhaps we do," agreed Alethea happily, "and since Elizabeth went away the gentlemen who attend them have more time for *us*."

"Oh, Alethea!" scolded Catherine, though not at all seriously. "If that is the case, we should be in the loggia now, being pleasant to John Lyford."

"You can go and do that, Catherine, and I shall sit here

and eat ices with my friends."

"How droll you are, Alethea."

Jane watched this sisterly exchange with recognition, thinking of Elizabeth, who had so often led similar ones. "Catherine, you must miss your sister since she became Mrs Heathcote," she observed. Saying this name was a test she had set herself, which she passed easily. She did not colour. Her attraction to Elizabeth's husband had disappeared that Christmas-time in this very house, upon the instant that Tom Lefroy had smiled at her.

Catherine shrugged. "A little, but we have each other. You must not compare our situation with your own."

Jane ate a spoonful of her ice. "Yes, I do miss Cass," she admitted when she had recovered from the shock of its coldness against her teeth. "But luckily, I am able to create my own companions in her absence."

"Of course you are!" Catherine clapped her hands ecstatically. "What are you writing now? Do tell us! What is the name of your heroine?"

Jane took a breath to tell her, but the word turned into a laugh. "Why, Catherine, the name of my new heroine is … *Catherine*!"

Catherine grinned with pleasure. "And what happens to her?"

"I have not yet worked it out. But I have a mind to set it in a place I have not used before."

"Switzerland?" asked Alethea, round-eyed. "In a lonely castle on a rock?"

"Jane does not write novels like the silly ones you read," admonished Catherine.

"Actually," began Jane, "this novel will, I think, bear some homage to Alethea's favourite reading, which, by the way, Alethea, I do not consider silly at all."

"You see?" said Alethea to her sister with triumph.

"Though my setting is not Switzerland," continued Jane. "I am considering a place much nearer home, since my family are to travel there in a few weeks."

Martha had heard about this plan, probably from Mary. "Oh, yes! You are all to go to Bath, I gather."

"Indeed," said Jane, spooning up some more of her ice. "Are you not envious?"

Alethea and Catherine, who enjoyed their visits to Bath greatly, replied that they were. But Martha knew that Jane had spoken ironically. "I predict that you will enjoy your stay in 'that infamous watering-hole', as Madam Lefroy calls it, far better than last time," she said.

"Why?" asked Jane, surprised. "Bath has not changed."

"But *you* have, Jane. You are not seventeen any more, but a woman of twenty-three, and your distaste for late supper parties and over-subscribed public balls may well have diminished. There is no disputing the potential of Bath as a place of love and intrigue, and therefore highly suitable for a novel's setting. But you may find those very things invaluable in real life."

Jane was unconvinced. "The people of Bath, then, are to be so fortunate as to witness my next skirmish with the world of husband-seeking, are they?"

"Yes, indeed," retorted her friend. "And you shall have no Cass to hold your cloak while you enter the fray!"

"What shall you do with your hair?" asked Alethea. She leaned nearer Jane, scrutinizing her curls. "Such pretty hair, but you always wear it so plainly dressed, Jane."

"What style of pinning up, or trailing down, or heaven-knows-what-else is fashionable in Bath?" Jane asked her. "I suppose it will not do to excite gossip at the Pump Room about my old-fashioned clothes or country hairstyle, interesting though that would be."

"No, indeed," agreed Alethea solemnly. "Everyone in Bath is smartly dressed all the time, even in the mornings, are they not, Catherine? When we went there, the three of us and Mama had more than thirty gowns between us, and it still was not enough. I came back with rents in at least five of mine, from dancing."

"It becomes so crowded," added Catherine, by way of explanation. "Where shall you be staying?"

"With my uncle and aunt. Mama is looking forward to gathering a large family party in her brother's house."

"How delightful!" exclaimed Alethea. "Are you not excited?"

Jane was not. Ever since it had first been proposed, her spirits had dipped whenever the visit to Bath was mentioned. She knew she must, for her mother's sake, enter into the life of the fashionable spa town with good grace, however much she longed to be at home tending her vegetables.

"I do not think so," she told Alethea. "But I suppose if I take *Catherine* with me, I shall enjoy myself in my own way."

The crowd in the Bath Assembly Rooms was as heedless of ladies' garments as Alethea had described. Each time Jane attended she had to mend a hem, or the fringe of a shawl, the next morning. Her shoes were trodden on, her stockings dirtied; even her favourite fan, a present from her brother Frank, was knocked to the floor one night and trampled by the dancers before she could rescue it.

She knew that the people she met dismissed "Miss Austen" – neither pretty nor plain, accompanied by a sharp-eyed mother and an indulgent father – as yet another husband-hungry girl. But they did not, to her unutterable satisfaction, know that Miss Austen went back to her uncle's house every night and wrote by candlelight.

Catherine was taking shape very satisfactorily. Catherine Morland, as she had decided to name the heroine, was seventeen years old when the story began. From the instant Martha had observed that Jane herself had visited Bath for the first time at that age, the character had begun to create itself. Jane had merely to bundle up the many pleasant but undoubtedly "girlish" girls she knew, and tie up the bundle with Catherine Morland's particular traits: hair that would not curl without papers, a face described by Mr Morland as "almost pretty", and a keen interest in reading dramatic poetry as well as novels of unstinting horror.

Bath society fulfilled all Jane's expectations of satirical opportunities. She set down its whims and foibles, its wit and lack of it, its wigs and snuffboxes and feathers and fans. She took Catherine Morland shopping the length of Milsom Street. She took her to the theatre, the concert-hall, the Assembly Rooms and the "watering-places", introducing her to the people who would provide the story. A young man, of course, and another rival young man, and a lively girl designed to make Catherine feel her own social shortcomings. Then she took her to stay at an ancient abbey, exactly like the heroines of a dozen novels whose chief intention was to terrify the reader. But instead of Catherine's bravery being tested by supernatural events at Northanger Abbey, her expectations were confounded by the very ordinariness of the place.

Jane was lost in writing. Sometimes, just before they ventured out in the morning, her mother would catch her turning this way and that before the looking-glass. She would accuse her, approvingly, of learning the insufferably vain ways of Bath ladies. Jane, however, would not have been admiring her reflection at all, but weighing up possibilities in her imagination. Did Catherine wear her bonnet bow in the centre, like Jane herself, or to the side? Would Catherine have a silk parasol for daywear, or only in the evening? Would she accept an invitation to go for a carriage-ride with a young man, chaperoned, of course, or would she be too shy? The character had ceased to be merely a means for creating a comic story. Like Marianne and Elizabeth before her, Catherine had entered Jane's profound, secret self.

Upon their arrival home from Bath, Cass was also back at Steventon, Elizabeth having been safely delivered of another boy. When everyday life had settled around Jane again, she showed the half-written manuscript to her sister.

"Why, Jane, how busy you have been!" exclaimed Cass. "And yet you wrote nothing last summer in Kent. I was convinced that even after I had my coloured dresses made you were not going to adhere to your side of our bargain."

"I could not think of anything to write," confessed Jane. She paused, decided to add something, changed her mind, then said it anyway. "To own the truth, Cass, the rejection from Cadells was hard to bear. I wondered for a while if the publishing business is too intimidating for a mere rector's daughter to enter. But when I came back to Steventon the writing-desk – and the chair with that cushion you made for it, and Edward's old pen-wipers, and all my own things – seemed to speak to me, and tell me to start something new. I had the idea of looking over some old manuscripts, and found *Lady Catherine*. Do you remember it?"

"I do indeed!" laughed Cass. "A great deal befell that poor young lady in a few pages, if I am not mistaken. Have you changed it much?"

"I have used nothing except the name," admitted Jane, "and she has lost her title. She is plain Catherine Morland now, one of a large family like ours, but otherwise, I think, not much like us. She is too much influenced by sensational novels, which neither of us would ever admit to being, of course."

Cass's eyes scanned the first page. They began to shine. "Oh, Jane! Your writing improves with everything I read."

Jane did not reply, though she felt grateful for this response from her sister, never her most severe critic, but not an indulgent one either.

"I adore Catherine already," declared Cass, reading on. "If she considers herself 'in training for a heroine' – how sweet! – then I have every confidence she will prove delightful. How artless and eager for life she is! She almost makes me wish to be seventeen again myself."

"This is only half of the first draft," protested Jane. Her heartbeat had quickened. She had written that first short chapter on a rainy night in Bath, when everyone else had gone to the theatre and she had pleaded a sore throat. It had taken perhaps an hour to write, another hour to revise. And here was Cass reading part of it aloud, and praising it as any newspaper critic might praise a new writer's work. "I must admire your perception, Cass," she continued.

"Catherine is exactly as you say, artless and eager."

"It is not my *perception* that has made her so," said Cass in exasperation, "it is your *talent*."

Jane smiled her pleasure. "Thank you, dearest. I shall soon finish it, and then it will need some revision, but perhaps I can present it to Papa in a few months, and see what he thinks."

"Any simpleton can predict what he will think."

By the time the autumn arrived, *Catherine* was finished. It lay in the drawer, much crossed and blotted, during the last months of 1799. Dramatic news from Europe had made its way to Steventon: Admiral Nelson's rout of the French navy at the Battle of the Nile had lifted everyone's spirits, but Bonaparte, undeterred, had now seized power, and become the ruler of France. Often during that chilly, blustery season, Jane and Cassandra put on their capes and muffs and walked in the lanes around Steventon, sometimes visiting parishioners but more likely merely passing the time together.

Passing the time. Jane imagined the nineteenth century as a stony path twisting to an invisible horizon. Would she and Cass still be walking between these hedges in ten, twenty, thirty years time, leaning on each other for physical, as well as moral, support?

"Papa says the true start of the nineteenth century is not until January eighteen hundred and *one*," Cassandra observed on the way home from church one wet Sunday. "He says eighteen hundred is actually the last year of the eighteenth century, which logic decrees is correct, you know."

"Logic never yet made any impression upon public perception," replied Jane, stepping round a puddle. "The world wishes eighteen hundred to be the start of the new century, and the world shall have its way."

"True," sighed Cassandra.

"But you know, Cass, I do find myself wondering, at this special time, what the future holds."

"God has made His plans already, and His servants must accept them," mused Cass. "Frank and Charles are still away, and Papa and Mama are becoming older. Did you notice last evening that Mama could not read the newspaper even with her spectacles on? And Papa is forever falling asleep in the middle of sentences."

"His habit is to sit too near the fire," said Jane. "The heat makes him soporific. But at least since the school closed he no longer has to employ his energies in teaching."

"Do you miss the boys?" Cassandra asked unexpectedly.

Jane thought. "I confess I do not miss the extra work they made; but the advantage of the boys was that their families became known to us. Our circle of acquaintance has shrunk since they left."

Cassandra was silent for a long time. Jane, with a stab of embarrassment, wished her words unsaid. Cass had met Tom Fowle because he had been one of Papa's pupils, as had all his brothers. The Fowles had heard of the school in the first place because they were related to Mrs Lloyd's late husband, and in those days the Lloyds had lived close by at Deane. A circle of acquaintance was exactly that: connected, reliable, satisfyingly logical.

"I miss them, every one," murmured Cass at last.

Jane took her sister's elbow to guide her to the edge of the flooded lane. "Hold up your hem, dearest, or Kitty shall have to dry and brush our clothes."

"She shall be attending to Mama's without doubt," Cass declared, indicating their mother, who walked ahead of them, allowing her cloak and skirt to trail in the muddy water. "But she is used to it, thank the Lord."

Papa was excited about the passing of the old century and the birth of the new one. He planned special New Year celebrations and a thanksgiving service at Steventon Church.

"What exactly are we giving thanks for?" asked Henry, who had arrived one afternoon with the news that he had left the militia and was about to embark on a financial career in the City of London.

"We are giving thanks for my long and happy life as vicar of this parish," explained Papa. "I am not far off seventy years old, Henry, and as my parishioners insist this is the turn of the century, it seems an appropriate occasion on which to reflect on years past and years to come."

Jane was sitting in the inglenook sewing a nightgown for Mary's little James-Edward. Her stitches were fine, but sewing strained her eyes. She put down her work and joined the conversation. "Shall you bring Eliza for Christmas, Henry? We have not seen her for a long time."

"Sadly, no," replied Henry. "We have a long-standing invitation to visit her friends in the north country."

"Do they wish to inspect her husband, in case he is unsuitable?"

"If he were, there is little they could do, two years after the wedding," observed Henry. He gave Jane one of his bright-eyed looks, which always reminded her why he was her favourite brother, and why Eliza had preferred him to James.

"I am persuaded you will charm them, Henry, as you

charm everybody," she said. "Now, tell me, how do you get on in the City?"

"Tolerably."

"Do you go out to business every day, in a black coat and hat, carrying your papers in a leather case like an attorney? I should like to see it."

"No, I do not," he told her solemnly, his eyes still bright. "My associates and I meet whenever it is necessary, to discuss our affairs and contract business. And I have been known to wear striped breeches in the City as, indeed, anywhere else."

Papa leaned forward in his chair, amused. "Striped breeches? And a silk cravat?"

"Exactly so, sir. I leave the wearing of sober attire to my brother James, who was ever more serious than I."

Jane's birthday passed like the previous one, in cold weather and with all her brothers away from home. The only difference was that Cass was "being with" Elizabeth at Godmersham in the expectation of another confinement, and Jane had to dress her own chilblains and brush her own hems. It was always cold in the Rectory, but that winter seemed colder than ever, and lonely. No schoolboys, no brothers, no Cass. Martha was too far away, at Ibthorpe, for daily visits. Most heavy upon Jane's heart, though, lay the conviction that when Tom Lefroy had returned to Ireland he had taken her future with him.

She tried scolding herself, accusing herself bitterly of over-exaggeration, self-regard, self-pity. But it did not work. If another man should ever love her enough to propose, and if she should ever love him enough – as much as Elizabeth loved Darcy – it would be a miracle. And then she would scold herself for her nonsensical habit of pretending her characters were real, and idealizing love between a man and a woman who had never actually existed. But where was Tom now, and did he ever think of her?

Mama seemed distracted, running from one place to another and changing her orders, exasperating Mrs Travers and Jane as well as the long-suffering Kitty. Visitors came and went: Madam Lefroy, slower on her legs now, with one or both of her sons; Alethea and Catherine, with or without their parents.

Martha, who was visiting her sister at Deane that November, appeared on her last morning at Steventon with Anna at her side and her little nephew James-Edward in her arms, ready to have Grandmama admire his two new teeth and indulge her grandchildren with bonbons and Christmas fruits.

Martha, meanwhile, insisted upon helping to add to the pile of baby clothes. "Your stitches are smaller than mine, Jane," she said, "but I am far better at smocking, so give me that pitiful piece you are working on. Here, you can hem this feeding-bib."

They sat in the upstairs sitting-room, listening to Anna's chatter and Papa's laughter through the floorboards. Jane's dread of encroaching solitude began to disperse; Martha's friendship, always welcome, seemed more invaluable now than ever before.

"Why not come back to Ibthorpe with me tomorrow?" Martha suggested. She tugged at the row of smocking, holding it up to the light. She did not look at Jane. "Mama will not mind, she loves you. Your company will enliven our quiet Christmas greatly."

Jane was sorely tempted to go to Ibthorpe and not come back until after Christmas, which would be equally as quiet at Steventon. She envied Cass, surrounded by children at Godmersham. Why could not Christmas be like it was when they were all at home, and had acted plays and taken provisions through the snow to the villagers?

"Martha, visiting Ibthorpe is exactly what I want to do, though I cannot stay for Christmas. Papa and Mama will expect me here."

"Then stay until just before. I shall put it to your parents before I go back to Deane this evening. We shall have so much opportunity to talk, and you know I always love to hear about everything you are writing."

"Dear Martha." Jane put out her hand and grasped her friend's. "Your intuition is so extraordinary. I believe you should go on the stage as a mind-reader, and I will join you as the accomplice who pretends to be a member of the audience. We could run away to London and make our fortunes."

Martha did not let go of her hand. She looked at Jane with an expression of intense feeling. "If only we could, Jane," she said. "If only we could."

Anna

"We are moving to *Bath*?"

Jane echoed her mother's words, her voice full of dismay.

"Yes, it is quite settled!" trilled Mama. "Now, let Kitty take that wet bonnet. What dreadful weather we are having this year! I would rather have snow than rain, and I am persuaded you feel the same." She began to untie Jane's bonnet and take off her gloves, as if Jane were a child no older than Anna. "You see, Papa has decided to retire to somewhere more lively than Steventon. He is to give up the living here and pass it to James, so the old house will still be in the family, and kept by our dear Mary better than it ever was by your Mama."

Jane said nothing. Her mother looked at her sharply. "Did you hear me?"

"Yes, I heard you," said Jane in a small voice. She felt as if every drop of blood in her body had rushed to her head. "When are we to leave?"

"In May."

Christmas was three days away. Jane had just alighted from

the carriage on her return from Ibthorpe, where she had passed the happiest week she could remember for a long time. But in a mere five months from this moment, everything she had known and loved for her entire life would change.

"In May!" she cried. "Mama, why did you not tell me before?"

"Papa and I have not told any of you until now. Except James, of course."

Kitty appeared. "Bring tea for Miss Jane," Mama instructed her, handing her Jane's outdoor clothes. "Is this not exciting, my dear?" she asked Jane when Kitty had gone. "Are you not pleased at the prospect of living in a new place, and meeting new people? How busy we shall be! And everything on the doorstep, instead of a carriage-ride away. Most convenient for older people like Papa and me."

Mama chattered on as they sat down by the fire, but Jane only half heard her words. So Mary and James had known they were to inherit the living at Steventon, and the house that went with it, during Martha's visit only a few weeks ago. And Mary had said nothing. Jane could not suppress uncharitable feelings towards her. If such close relatives were prepared to act parts in order to keep important secrets, what hope was there for trust and honour between anyone?

"So we must pack up our belongings," Mama was saying. "We must begin as soon as Papa's thanksgiving has passed."

Jane began to listen more carefully. "Pack up our belongings?"

"Why, yes. James and Mary already have two children, and may have more. We cannot expect them to make room for things which are not theirs. When we visit, as I am sure we shall, it will be as their guests."

"Their guests? But Steventon is *our* home!" Jane's finger-nails dug into her palms. She was trying hard to be calm, but each announcement by Mama made this more difficult.

"Only until May, my dear," said Mama steadily. "You have always known that a clergyman's house belongs to his church, and he may only live in it until the next incumbent of the parish relieves him at his post."

Yes, Jane had always known it. But she had hoped to be mistress of her own house before this inevitable move took place. Leaving her childhood home would have been a wrench even upon her marriage, but to have to leave it in the company of Cassandra, Mama and Papa! Other daughters of clergymen faced the same disruption daily, but to leave *her* Steventon, *her* Rectory, *her* kitchen garden, and the upstairs sitting-room, and the inglenook by the fire! She glanced at the inglenook now, as she and her mother awaited tea. The firelight blurred.

"Mama," she said, blinking away her tears, "I cannot pretend that Bath is as attractive to me as it is to you and Papa. But Cass, who will be surprised as I am when she hears the plan, will acquiesce immediately. That is her way. And if Cass can tolerate this sudden change, then so must I. I only wish you and Papa had not kept it secret. It is more than a surprise – it is a shock."

Kitty entered, set down the tray, bobbed a curtsey and was gone. "A pleasant shock, though, surely?" said Mama, busy-ing herself among the cups. "We have been plotting it for weeks and weeks, you know. I confess I am very excited!"

Jane had not seen her mother so pleased since James and Mary's wedding. Her smile was irrepressible. She loved society and shopping, music and gossip. Now, after forty years as a country vicar's wife she had a chance to return to the more sophisticated life she had enjoyed as a girl. Could Jane could be so churlish as to deny her?

"Am I the first one to know?" she asked. "Apart from James and Mary?"

"You are," said Mama, handing her an over-full cup with too much milk in it. In forty years, she had never learnt to pour tea correctly. "Papa and I only heard this morning that the money for the rent in Bath is guaranteed, and since you were coming home today, I could not keep the news to myself any longer."

"When shall you tell the others?" asked Jane, sipping carefully.

"Oh, as and when," said her mother airily.

"Cass must be told soon, surely," said Jane, "as she and I are to be most affected. The others may be losing Steventon, but they are not moving from it."

"That is because they have moved from it already, my dear," declared Mama impatiently.

"Frank and Charles have not," retorted Jane. "Where shall they live, when they leave the navy?"

"They shall take wives, I imagine, and set up house with them," said Mama. She was no longer smiling. "Really, Jane, you must not take this so tragically. The house will be in James's hands, and that is that. You are a very lucky girl, to be taken to live in Bath, so near your uncle and aunt, with all their acquaintance."

There was nothing more to say. Jane drank her tea, told her mother she would write immediately to Cassandra, and walked slowly up to her sitting-room, conscious of every one of her footsteps on every one of the stairs, thinking, thinking…

The house in Bath would not be a house at all. It would be an apartment, with no more than four rooms. She and Cass would not have their own sitting-room with a fireplace and a window seat. Their bedroom would not overlook a much-loved garden but wet cobbles, passers-by and endless traffic. Opposite their window, instead of farm fields changing with the seasons, they would see someone else's apartment window. They would have to draw down their blind to avoid being observed by strangers. And it would be so not merely for the duration of a visit, but for the rest of their days.

Jane's head ached. Her limbs felt awkward; she could not move with her famous grace. She pulled out the carved chair. Was this treasured thing, so meaningful to Jane, so trivial to everyone else, to be left for *James and Mary*?

She sat down unsteadily at the writing desk where Catherine Morland had followed Elizabeth Bennet and the Dashwood sisters into the corners of her heart. She took a piece of paper and smoothed it with shaking fingers. But when she reached for a pen, her feelings overcame her. She could not write to Cass until she had collected herself.

But she could not collect herself. She sat for a long time, her feet in their outdoor boots crossed beneath the chair, her elbows on the desk, her head in her hands. Desperation rose up, and brought tears, but she went on sitting there. Hating herself for even considering the word, she told herself that this was a betrayal. And it had been committed by the very people who were supposed to love her.

Mama's enthusiasm she could comprehend, but Papa's was unfathomable. Why should he be ready to leave his parish at such short notice, and go so far away? He of all people – the champion of Jane's literary efforts, the defender of her observations, the wise circumnavigator of conflict with Mama. Why had he deserted his post when he was needed most?

Perhaps she was still seeing her father with a child's trust. But for whatever reason, he concurred with Mama's conviction that he had lived quietly for long enough, and that since he was no longer to serve the parish, there was no reason to live in it.

But *Bath*! Jane fetched a handkerchief and cried noisily into it. Unchristian though it might be, she could not help but pity herself and her sister. The helplessness of their situation was not merely unfair. It was demeaning.

She had never before been so strongly convinced of this. She and Cass had discussed Miss Wollstonecraft's *Vindication of the Rights of Women* when they had first read it, years ago. Cass had marvelled at the audacity of the suggestion that women should be educated to a high level and granted the opportunity to enter the professions, though to Jane this hypothesis had always seemed entirely correct. They had both laughed, however, when they had tried to picture a woman lawyer, in a wig and gown, or a woman Member of Parliament trying to make herself heard above the robust shouting in the House. Now, Jane's frustration at being moved to Bath as if she were a piece of furniture, with no possible alternative simply because she was an unmarried woman, overcame her so violently that she cast herself down upon the bed.

She wept for a long time. If only her sister were at home! Jane knew her sister-in-law needed Cassandra more than she did at present, but how she missed her! On this dreary winter evening, with the rain dribbling down the window-panes and the larches behind the house groaning in sympathy with her mood, Jane wished and wished for her sister to appear.

But it was the wish of a child. Jane's powers of reasoning told her that Cass could not return until Elizabeth could spare her, and that she had the advantage over her sister anyway. Unlike poor Cass, Jane did not have to spend their final weeks away from Steventon. While it was still their home, Jane could at least live in it.

"Where are you, Jane?"

It was Papa's voice. Jane wiped her face and went out onto the landing. "Here, Papa."

He was at the bottom of the stairs, smiling, with his whiskers brushed and his spectacles gleaming. Jane's heart swelled at the sight; he was as excited as a schoolboy. "What is it, Papa?"

"Mary and James are here."

Jane had no wish to see her brother or his wife. "Is Anna with them?"

"She is."

"Please may I have her up here?"

"I do not see why not." He disappeared, then reappeared holding his granddaughter by the hand. "Go up to your Aunt Jane, my child."

Still in her cape and bonnet, Anna trotted up the stairs. Jane sank to her knees and clasped the little girl tightly to her breast. More tears came, but she did not care; children understood tears. Anna would understand what had caused these, and disperse them as only children could.

"Aunt Jane, I cannot breathe."

Jane released the child. She took hold of both her hands and looked into the small face of the niece she loved best. "Anna dearest, come and help me write a letter to Aunt

Cassandra. I confess I know not where to start, but you always have the cleverest ideas."

"Why are you crying?" asked Anna, with troubled eyes.

Having been kept in ignorance herself, Jane was wary in case Anna had been too. "Have your Mama and Papa told you any news lately?"

"They told me something this morning."

"Yes, dearest? What did they say?"

"That Grandpapa is not going to be the vicar of Steventon any more, and we are to move from Deane and come to live here at the Rectory."

"That is quite true," said Jane, "and I must write and tell Aunt Cass. But I have a headache. Will you be a good girl and sit at the desk with me?"

"I shall be glad to," said Anna in her serious way. "Would you take off my gloves, please, Aunt? I cannot undo the buttons."

Jane obliged, sniffing back tears. And when the slender eight-year-old fingers were free, aunt and niece went hand-in-hand into the sitting-room. Together they composed a letter containing the most heart-breaking news Jane had ever had to impart to her sister, leavened only by the brightness of Anna's astonishment when Jane speculated that one day, perhaps, this very sitting-room and everything in it would be Anna's own.

"Why, Aunt Jane!" she exclaimed, her eyes and mouth equally wide open. "If I truly may sit on *your* chair, at *your* desk, one day … might I be an author, like you?"

The desk and chair remained at Steventon. But by the day of moving, Jane had no heart for regret at leaving them behind. She was not sure her heart was even in the same place as it had always been, or that she had any true feelings at all. Months of agreeing when inwardly she objected, smiling when she had no desire for merriment, tirelessly dusting and wrapping and packing when she longed for all the things to be left exactly where they were, had hardened her.

She resolved that she would not weep, or allow her parents to suspect the depth of her unhappiness. Leave she must, so leave she would, without demur.

"We must make of Bath what we can," Cassandra had said upon her return from Godmersham. "I cannot pretend to like the notion of James and Mary living in our house any more than you do, but since there is nothing we can do about it, we must do as the Bible commands. *Blessed are the meek.*"

Jane did not want to be meek, but she could no longer summon the rage of that first tearful hour. "Very well, Cass," she had agreed. "When required, I can be as meek as anyone else. But I am sure that meekness will not make me inherit the earth. I would rather inherit the Rectory anyway, which I cannot do because Papa does not own it, and even if he did, it would go to exactly the same person who is having it anyway. James!"

"Oh, Jane, do not dwell on the ways of the world," Cassandra had wisely advised. "It was ever a pointless exercise, and only makes for misery."

Mama and Papa had at least taken note of James's suggestion that they take a *house* in Bath, rather than an upstairs apartment. Jane did not know how to express her gratitude to her brother for this intervention. When she tried, he patted her hand and said, "I love Steventon in equal measure with all my sisters and brothers. When the time comes for me to leave it, if I do not live somewhere with room to move, and some greenery to look at, I shall die."

Jane might have been unable to thank James, but she thanked God when she saw their new house. It was a town house, certainly, in a row with many others. But it overlooked rarely used public gardens. The river was nearby, crossed by the impressive Poultney Bridge, and the house itself was large enough for Cassandra and Jane to have a private room. It even had a garden, "the size of a Bath bun" in Cassandra's opinion, which received enough sun for her lavender and Jane's lettuces to grow.

"You see," said Cassandra as they made ready for bed on the first night, "our situation is not so bad, is it?"

Jane had to admit she was right. "No, indeed. The sight of the city in the sunshine today has lightened my spirits considerably."

"I am glad to hear it," said Cassandra with relief. "How distressed you were, and how reasonable you are being now!"

"I am not Marianne Dashwood," said Jane.

"Which reminds me," said Cassandra. "Marianne Dashwood is in the box with Elizabeth Bennet and all the others, is she not? And the box is brought safely from Steventon, is it not? Well, now that you are in Bath again, you can revise *Catherine*, and perhaps start a new story."

"Perhaps," said Jane.

But the city of Bath did not yield the glorious immersion in fiction of her earlier sojourn there. *Catherine* stayed in the box, the paper on the writing table remained blank, and each day was so like the one before that the restlessness which descended upon Jane became almost too great to bear.

"I will die in this place," she told Cassandra one night. "I must have air. Cannot we prevail upon Mama and Papa to take us somewhere else?"

"Where do you suggest?"

"They are always saying they would like to visit Dorset. Lyme and Weymouth especially. Those places are by the sea, Cass. I could breathe there. Being here makes me feel as if I need … adventure."

"Adventure?" said Cass, stopping in her task of hair-curling.

"I daily feel my prospects closing. There is nothing here for me. We might even try Wales. What do you think?"

"You had better ask them," said Cass.

Jane's suggestion was enthusiastically supported by her parents. "If we go as far as Weymouth, my dears," suggested Papa, "we might as well go on to Hampshire and stay with James and Mary at Steventon. Mama and I can then come home, and you and your sister can go to Manydown. The Biggs are constantly inviting you. And you may also visit Martha at Ibthorpe."

Jane expressed her joy in long letters to Martha, Catherine and Alethea, but it was a short letter from Mrs Bigg which interrupted the pleasurable preparations for their journey. Three days before they were to leave for Weymouth, Mama plunged the breakfast table into horrified silence.

"Mrs Bigg writes to tell me that her daughter Elizabeth has been widowed."

Jane actually felt the blood drain from her cheeks, in a way often described in the kind of novels Catherine Morland liked to read, but which Jane had never believed could happen. Her breakfast turned to stone in her stomach as Papa and Cassandra questioned Mama, and the story was read out.

There was no mistake. William Heathcote, the charming,

reserved clergyman whose physical beauty had been the first to stir Jane's blood, had died of a sudden seizure a week previously. His young wife, bereft not only of her husband but of her house, which was provided by the Church, had immediately packed her bags and taken herself and her baby son back to live with her parents at Manydown House. Mrs Bigg was at pains to explain that Cassandra and Jane were welcome to visit as planned, but they would find Manydown in mourning for some weeks, and Elizabeth in black for many months beyond that.

"Then we shall change our plans," declared Papa.

"Oh, no, George!" begged Mama. "The girls are looking forward to seeing the Bigg girls so much."

"Exactly," said Papa. "I meant, we shall alter our itinerary, so that the girls do not arrive at Manydown until the autumn. Perhaps the Biggs will even reinstate their traditional Christmas ball, if two young lady guests are present at that season."

"I doubt it," said Mama. "Not this year, anyway."

Jane and Cass composed a letter to Elizabeth. Neither shed tears, and they did not speak, or write, of William Heathcote's death in any terms but the conventional ones. But Jane was dispirited by the memories his passing produced. The ball where Elizabeth Bigg had met her future husband had taken place in a world now irrevocably lost to both Cassandra and herself: a world where Tom Fowle was still alive, where Tom Lefroy remained unsuspecting of Jane's existence, where "the Johns" − Lyford, Portal, Harwood − and many other young gentlemen had clustered around the punch bowl and swung their partners more and more exuberantly as the punch disappeared. It was a long time ago, and everything since then had changed.

Harris

The visit to James and Mary at Steventon Rectory turned out better than Jane had expected. As summer turned into autumn the weather remained unseasonably warm, and her parents were able to spend the afternoons visiting many of their old parishioners with James, Mary and their grandchildren.

It was on one of these afternoons that Madam Lefroy drove over unannounced from Ashe. Less sprightly than of old, but exactly the same in every other detail, she was shown by Kitty into the garden, where Jane and Cass were sitting in the sunshine. Jane, as ever, was reading, and Cassandra sewing.

"What do you think, my dears? What do you *think*? And how do you go along in Bath, by the way?" asked Madam Lefroy. "Reverend Lefroy never could abide the place, though I am not averse to it; do not tell him, poor man."

"Will you not sit down, Madam?" asked Cass, offering her own chair to the visitor. "Kitty, please bring another chair from the kitchen."

Madam Lefroy sat down and settled herself as solidly as if she would never move. "What an obliging girl that is," she observed as Kitty ran into the kitchen. "If she ever wants to give Mrs James notice she would be heartily welcome at Ashe. So, what do you say to my news?"

Cassandra reminded her tactfully that she had not told them it.

"Why, it is about my nephew, Mr Tom Lefroy!"

Jane's heart leapt with such a bound she had to put her hand to her breast. She could not breathe until Madam Lefroy spoke again. If Tom had indeed been permitted to return, Jane was convinced she would kneel without embarrassment at Madam's feet, and kiss the hem of her gown. She could not look at Cassandra.

"Thank you, Kitty," said Cass calmly. She sat down and took up her work again. "And is your nephew well?"

"I should say he is *very* well," replied Madam Lefroy. "My dears, he has made *such* an advantageous marriage! Quite an heiress, I understand. An Irishwoman, very pleasing to the eye by all accounts. But then he always was a very presentable young man himself."

Madam's eyes settled upon Jane. She met them briefly, but she could not continue to observe the determined carelessness she saw there. Dispirited, she kept her eyes on the book in her lap.

It was almost seven years since the Christmas ball at Manydown where Jane and Tom had met. The Irish Lefroys' all-too-obvious fear that Tom would marry Jane had embarrassed Madam Lefroy so much that she had been unable to face the Austens for months, and she had not allowed the name of Tom Lefroy to pass her lips in Jane's presence for years. But now, so anxious was she to impress upon the Austen family the excellence of Tom's match, such considerations seemed forgotten. Jane was too crushed to reply.

"An Irish lady, you say?" replied the socially skilful Cassandra. "And where in Ireland do they live?" She led Madam Lefroy away from Tom's marriage to his new house, and from there to his honeymoon journey, and from there to the Austens' own travels in Dorset. And all the time Jane stared at the book, her brain beset by visions. The way Tom had flipped his coat-tails when they "sat out" between dances. The joy and indulgence upon people's faces a week later at Ashe, when he and she had opened the dancing. The hair pushed impatiently back from his brow, his wrists in their starched frills, the neat closure of one boot against the other as he completed the measures. And especially that most cherished sight of all, his bright yet tender smile.

"Will you perhaps come and visit us in Bath, Madam?" Cassandra was asking.

"Oh, no, my poor legs will not allow me the luxury of travel these days, thank you all the same. But, Miss Jane, you are very quiet."

Jane had to look up. But her throat had contracted; it was difficult to speak. Uncaring that she was being impolite, she stood up. "Madam," she said, with a brief curtsey, "I am sorry, but I … I feel most unwell. Please excuse me."

"Of course, my dear," said Madam Lefroy in dismay, but without bewilderment. "As you wish. That excellent housemaid will bring you your tea upstairs, I dare say."

Jane did not want any tea. Madam Lefroy sat with Cassandra a long time, while Jane lay on the bed and stared at the wallpaper, dry-eyed, silent, thinking. When she heard the carriage pull away she returned to the garden, where Cass sat with her head on a cushion and her work abandoned.

"You are weary, Cass," said Jane, sitting on the grass at her sister's feet. "You have had a sorry afternoon of it. Please forgive me for deserting you. "

"It does not matter," said Cass. "In your shoes I would have done the same."

"I did not cry, though."

"What did you do?"

"I thought about money, marriage and men. I thought about the things men do. It gave me little comfort, but neither would crying, so it was of little consequence. What else did Madam say? I hope she did not press you to divulge the reason for my distress."

"I believe she had no need," said Cass. "She did speak of you, however. She wished to know what story you are working on these days."

"Infernal curiosity of the woman! And what did you tell her?"

"I said I did not know."

"Quite right."

There was a long pause, during which Jane pulled up blades of grass and dropped them, concentrating on the task as if it were very important.

"I will never write anything again," she said at last.

"Oh, please do not say that," sighed Cass.

"But I have not written a single word since we moved to Bath."

"That is because we have been so busy. And Bath is so frantic. Perhaps one day we shall settle in a house in the country somewhere, and you shall return to your writing."

"Perhaps you can tell me where such a house will appear from? Though even if it did appear, that is no guarantee of anything. My urge to write – as strong as the urge to breathe, I once said to –" she paused, "to Tom – has gone."

Cassandra did not speak. Jane was aware of her sister's watchful concern, and her own smarting eyes, but her voice was steady. "Perhaps, after all, I am an old-fashioned girl who simply likes to sit in this old-fashioned garden and read. Perhaps the pursuit of a literary career would bring me nothing but unhappiness. You must not take my words seriously. I am happy with my lot."

"I shall take your words as they are meant," said Cass. "You wish to write, but cannot, and you would rather blame yourself than our parents, whose desire to rush off to Bath like a couple of young puppies disturbed your peace so violently."

"And yours," said Jane.

"We are not speaking of me."

As impetuously as if they were children again, Jane put her head on her sister's lap. "Dearest, dearest Cass!"

They sat in silence among the long shadows. From the house came voices and kitchen noises. Someone went by on a horse and exchanged a greeting with Dick, who entered the garden by the back gate and sauntered round to the stable.

Finally Jane lifted her head. "Do you know what I am inclined to do?

"What?"

"Marry the first man who asks me, whoever he is."

Cass was dismayed "Even if you do not love him?"

Jane shook her head. "By Christmas I shall be twenty-seven. That is no age to be worrying about love." She let out an unamused laugh. "Indeed, I am exactly the age of Charlotte Lucas in *First Impressions*, when she married Elizabeth's rejected suitor, the absurd Mr Collins."

"Do you mean you will marry Mr Blackall, who is almost as absurd?" asked Cass, horrified.

"I am speaking of possibilities, Cass."

"But Charlotte Lucas and Mr Collins did not love each other at all," protested Cass. "And do you not remember how Charlotte's marriage distressed Elizabeth? She could not forgive her."

"I am not Elizabeth Bennet."

Cass gripped her sister's hand. "You are not Charlotte Lucas either; you are real. Do not be hasty. Pray do not make yourself unhappy for the sake of securing your own household. It would break my heart."

"When I created Charlotte Lucas," mused Jane, "I was twenty years old, and twenty-seven seemed impossibly old. Indeed, I wondered if I should make her younger, so as to make her situation less pathetic! But twenty-seven has arrived all too quickly, and no one – not even Mr Blackall – has proposed to me."

She stood up and brushed the grass from her skirt. "Come, let us go into the house and wait for them all to come home. We shall have a merry evening, our last one at Steventon for the present. We are to go to Ibthorpe tomorrow, and from there to Manydown. How pleasant it will be to see all our friends again! And if I cannot write, at least I can practise my powers of coquetry. If I do not find *someone* during all our travels, then I am a sorry specimen who does not deserve to marry, for love or anything else."

* * *

Jane and Cass, after a month at Ibthorpe, had brought Martha to stay at Manydown with them. Everyone was there: Alethea and Catherine, their brother Harris, who had now become a well-groomed young man of twenty-two, and tragic, still-beautiful Elizabeth.

Harris was now old enough to play a role in his family's unusually gracious hospitality. He was attentive to Jane, Cass and Martha, handing them from carriages, fetching shawls, offering amusements and outings. But Jane had not been at Manydown more than a week before she began to notice that he was particularly attentive to *her*.

It was October. Not a very mild October, but a dry one. Manydown was a glorious place to be when the leaves were turning, and the chestnut avenue behind the house was Jane's favourite walk. In the mornings, or after dinner when the rest of the household was at cards, which she did not care for, Harris walked with her there. No one considered the idea of accompanying them; they were childhood friends.

As a child Harris Bigg had had trouble with his speech, Jane recalled. For many years he had stammered, and was inclined not to make much contribution to conversation. She remembered him as a boy full of spirit, always ready to spar with one of the Lefroy boys, or slide recklessly on a polished floor, or risk broken limbs climbing trees and sledding. His father had not sent him to a public school, and, kept at home with his sisters, he had achieved a degree of understanding of the world of women Jane had only seen before in Charles Fowle. Both, as boys, had allowed girls into their games, and both, as men, could be trusted to put the hood of the carriage up when it was too windy for a feminine hairstyle, and not complain when kept waiting by a lengthy feminine toilette.

Harris did not stammer now. As they walked between the chestnuts he told her of his plans for Manydown, which his father had hinted might pass to him early, as he and Mrs Bigg were inclined to copy the Austens and go travelling.

"It is a fine old house, but some of the upstairs rooms need improvement," he said, stopping and indicating windows on the upper corner of the building. "These days a man must provide better quarters for his servants than of old. My father, sadly, does not understand this, and so my mother continues to complain that her maids do not stay long."

While they walked on, Jane looked at him. He was of more than middle height, and well-made without being thick-set. His hair was brown like hers. It looked as if it might soon thin at the temples, but she did not mind that. She had always liked the playful boy he had been when they had danced together at weddings, balls and house parties, and she had taught him to play the card-games she now despised. And she liked the man he had become.

What was more, he seemed to like her. One early December morning, when a cold mist lay on the ground and a walk was impossible, he forwent his usual ride in favour of joining Jane in the library. She wished to look at a book on a high shelf; he pushed the ladder into place, and would have climbed it for her if she had allowed him.

"It is all right, Harris, I have legs, you know."

He coloured immediately. Amused, yet flattered, Jane realized she could not speak of such intimate objects to a man whose amorous feelings were becoming daily more clear.

He went to the table and opened the nearest book which lay there, trying to cover his confusion. Jane did not like to see him discomfited. She did not climb the ladder, but joined him at the table.

"You have been very attentive to my sister, my friend and me since we have been here, for which I thank you," she said gently. "Martha in particular has remarked upon your pleasant company."

"It is not Miss Lloyd — I mean, I am much obliged to you," was his reply. His face was still rosy, and Jane had a notion that he was struggling against a temporary return of his stammer.

"Miss Lloyd is to be taken back to Ibthorpe on Friday, I understand," said Jane, only vaguely conscious that she should be saying something that put him at his ease, but in fact was succumbing to an almost mischievous desire to test him. "And Cass and I shall rejoin our parents in Bath later that day. And today is Tuesday."

"Yes," said Harris, without looking at her. He fingered the pages of the book. He was calmer now; his voice was steady. "My parents intend to give a small farewell party for you and your companions on Thursday evening." He raised his eyes to hers. "There will be dancing, I believe."

"In that case, I shall look forward to it greatly."

"Will you do me the honour of dancing with me?"

There was no need for such formality, but Jane recognized that Harris needed to show himself to be sensible of the rules of courtship. That he wished to court her was astonishing enough — she was, after all, his senior by five years, and a lifelong close friend of his older sisters — but his impeccable attention to courtesy and propriety lent his suit more weight than he could know. He would not break his promise like William Heathcote, or disappear across the sea like Tom Lefroy.

And he was the only male heir, the sole inheritor of Manydown.

"The honour will be all mine," she said, equally formally.

Suddenly he laughed, and slapped his palm on the table. "I feel as if I have had a glass of wine already!" he said, so ingenuously that Jane could not help but laugh too.

"Are you as good a dancer as you were when you were a little boy?" she asked.

"Better, I should hope! My sisters and I had lessons from a master. I can even do a minuet."

"The necessity for that will not arise, I am sure," replied Jane. "But I will join you in a reel, if you have the energy."

"Have you ever known me not have energy? *You* will be the one who begs to sit down, not I."

On Thursday evening Manydown House, though not decked out as splendidly as it had been for that important Christmas ball seven years before, felt warm and welcoming. Mr and Mrs Bigg's supper-dance, given for the family and a few friends, was necessarily subdued by Elizabeth's bereavement earlier in the year. But upon the instant Jane entered the familiar ballroom she detected an atmosphere of satisfaction, as if the Biggs were convinced that although some things had gone wrong, other things were about to go right.

"Everyone is smiling tonight," Jane remarked to Catherine. "Your family is very good at making guests welcome."

"I know," agreed Catherine. "Sometimes I wish I could be a guest myself." She threw Jane a coy look. "Do you ever wish you could be member of our family, Jane?"

Jane could not find an answer. She gazed at her friend,

too surprised even to blush. Were the events of the past few weeks so obvious to everyone?

"Oh, Jane, do not pretend that you have not noticed the attention that Harris has been paying you," said Catherine, snapping her fan closed and giving Jane a "really!" look.

"He is kind to everyone," said Jane blankly, her thoughts racing.

"He likes you, and you know it. He is always saying how clever you are, and how pretty your hair is."

"My hair?" repeated Jane.

"The very same."

"I am astonished."

"No, you are not. Alethea and I saw you through the library windows the other day when we were waiting for Stevens to bring the carriage round. You were laughing at everything he said." Catherine leaned nearer to Jane. In her eyes Jane saw hope, and concern, and affection. "Do not dismiss him if he should speak tonight, I beg of you. He is young and easily bruised."

Jane could hardly keep herself from smiling. She realized with a rush of joy that Catherine and her family were as desirous of the attachment as Harris himself.

"Now you must excuse me," said Catherine. "My mother is signalling to me."

Jane remained where she was standing, her imagination working. If Harris *did* speak tonight, which last Tuesday had seemed scarcely possible, Jane would leave tomorrow as the future mistress of the house she now stood in. After her marriage she would have not only Manydown, but a carriage and a barouche, like Edward and Elizabeth. She would have a housekeeper and several indoor and outdoor servants, housed in quarters improved by her husband's good sense. Her sons would be educated at public schools, and her daughters at home with a governess.

Her words about accepting the next man who asked her had surely been prophetic. Had God been listening? Was the inheritance due for her meekness over the move to Bath about to come in the form of Harris Bigg?

"Our dance, Miss Jane?"

Harris stood before her, his hand outstretched. She curtseyed low and accepted his hand. He drew her hand to his breast. "I cannot tell you how much pleasure this affords me," he said *sotto voce*, his eyes alight.

This was bold, and very romantic. Jane was overwhelmed; her colour rose, she smiled widely. "Why, thank you, Harris," she whispered.

She walked with him to the set. She tried her very best not to allow Tom Lefroy into her consciousness, but he *would* come. He had trodden these very floorboards with a twenty-year-old girl so delighted by his presence she could not feel her feet. Seven years later, Harris Bigg now turned to face the less idealistic woman she had become. He looked solemn, nervous, knowing he held his destiny by the hand.

During the dance he did not speak. She was half aware that people were watching and whispering about them, but she did not mind. It was clear that Harris's mind was working furiously as he completed the measures and turns. Cass had to skip out of the way to avoid a collision when he momentarily forgot in which direction he was supposed to proceed. He smiled ruefully, but was unembarrassed. And when the music had finished and the dancers were applauding he led Jane to the flagstoned loggia at the back of the house. He made no attempt to sit down, or to invite her to do so. As soon as they were out of earshot of the merrymakers he took her hands.

"Jane … I may call you Jane, may I not?"

"By all means," said Jane, so quietly that she barely heard herself. She could not breathe properly.

"Jane, I planned to say this after the last dance, not the first, but I cannot contain my desire to speak now."

She said nothing. Encouraged by her lack of protest, he continued.

"You can have no doubt that over the past few weeks I have developed an attachment to you, which I hope most sincerely might be returned."

Again Jane did not speak. She could hear his tense, shallow breathing. She gave a slight nod.

"Tell me," he said, his brown eyes bright, "if I may have the further honour of hoping that you will consider a proposal I have in mind."

Jane felt as if she were back in the drawing-room at Steventon, dressed in her mother's old clothes, acting in a play with Henry, while Cass and the other boys waited, giggling, behind a curtain. "Of course," she said softly.

"Then…" He swallowed, and his eyes filled with an expression whose like she had only seen once before, in Tom Lefroy's. "Then, will you bestow upon me the greatest happiness I can imagine, and consent to marry me, Jane?"

Jane had written several proposals in her books, some accepted, some rejected, some comic, some serious. But Harris's proposal was not like any she had written. He had approached her so directly, with such an attractive combination of bashfulness and desire in his countenance, that the possiblity of eloquence did not enter her head.

"Yes, Harris, I will."

She had barely uttered the words before he had gathered her to him and kissed her, not quite on the lips, but somewhere very near. Jane clung to him, her brain on fire. She had done what she had promised Cassandra she would do. She had accepted the first man who asked her. It was done. She was engaged.

"Let us announce our engagement now!" he said, releasing her at last.

She had never seen greater pride on the face of a young man. Grinning, he led her back to the ballroom. Mr Bigg did not have to hear the news; he saw it on their countenances as soon as they entered. With a glance he communicated it to his wife and daughters, and before she knew it Jane was being toasted with champagne.

"Our wish come true!" exclaimed Mrs Bigg, gazing fondly at her. "We have always longed for this moment, my dear. You have made us very happy."

Jane sipped, and then gulped, a glass of champagne, and then another. The dancing began again, food and wine appeared, midnight passed. Martha and the Bigg girls cried, but Cass remained dry-eyed. She said little, but kissed Jane warmly. Jane, who knew her sister better than anyone, was sure that she was deeply moved by her younger sister's success, but needed assurance that Jane's feelings for Harris were genuine. *Tomorrow*, Jane determined, *when we can be alone again, I will give her that assurance*.

Very late, she and Cass made their way up the carpeted staircase to their separate rooms. "Oh, Cass, I do love you," Jane said impulsively as they parted at her door.

"And I you, dearest. Now go to sleep, and look beautiful for your fiancé tomorrow morning."

Jane kissed her and went into the bedroom. Catherine's maid had laid out her night things and turned down the bedclothes. Jane washed her face and curled her hair untidily, hardly noticing what she was doing. Her limbs felt heavy as she changed, shivering, into her nightdress. She was fatigued beyond description. It was with relief that she climbed into bed and closed her eyes, and waited for the blankets to warm her.

But she did not sleep. She opened her eyes and looked at the stars between the open curtains, thinking, thinking...

A name drifted into her mind, and out again, and in again. Charlotte Lucas. Charlotte Lucas. Charlotte Lucas. And Cassandra's words: "do not make yourself unhappy ... it would break my heart."

Time passed, and Jane's thoughts cleared. Harris Bigg would be a perfect husband. Rich, kind, a member of a loving and beloved family. As a father to her children he would be more than perfect: educated at home like her own brothers, he had grown up surrounded by domestic concerns; he understood children. As a child himself, his ability to extract fun out of the most unpromising materials had ever impressed her. And now he would do the same for her own sons and daughters, and they would adore him.

She thought about Elizabeth Bigg, whose husband's untimely death had wrenched her from her happiness. She would not remarry, Jane suspected. Her boy, who at two years old had so much of his father's looks and ways it was almost distressing to see, would be the centre of her future existence. And at least she *had* him. If she had never been married, she would never have been widowed, but neither would she have her son. There was no doubt, Jane reasoned, that in view of the unexpected dangers of the world, marrying Harris and having his children was the rational thing to do.

But Charlotte Lucas's justification for marrying Mr Collins was that it was rational. What Elizabeth Bennet recoiled from, Charlotte sacrificed herself to. In making her do this, Jane's intention was to show readers – if anyone was ever going to read *First Impressions*, which was not at all certain – that a rational marriage was not the same as a love-match.

She sat up suddenly. There was no denying it. Not only was a rational marriage not the same as a love-match, it was *inferior*. And she had known that even when she was twenty years old, when she created Charlotte Lucas.

She threw off the covers and sat on the edge of the bed. The cold was intense. Reaching for her robe, she huddled in it, shivering and thinking.

If Charlotte Lucas was a realist, then Elizabeth Bennet was surely an *idealist* in her refusal to applaud Charlotte's decision. Jane had been on Elizabeth's side then. But by the age of twenty-seven, had she, Jane, not become a realist like Charlotte? And she was not even making the same sacrifice, since Harris Bigg was very far from being a Mr Collins. So why had the euphoria disappeared, and been replaced by this vast doubt which weighed on her, almost crushing her, as heavy as a stone?

It was almost morning. But it was midwinter; no gleam of dawn yet lit the room. Jane walked about, her slippers silent on the thick carpet, thinking, thinking...

What had she truly seen when Harris had looked at her? Had she seen what was actually there, or had she only seen what she hoped was there – the love she had mourned for seven years? Tom had secured his Irish heiress. But whoever he was married to, and however much he did or did not love his wife, he still belonged to Jane, and she to him. He still possessed her, even in memory, with a strength of feeling she could not summon for Harris or any other man. Tom's slight frame, his expressive eyes, his bony fingers and floppy hair, and his irrepressible air of joy had touched her heart with a power whose excitement she could not rid herself of, were she to try for the rest of her life.

She would have to admit the truth, first to herself then to the world. However suitable Harris was as a husband, and however tenderly he might love her, when he looked at her she saw another pair of eyes, lit by a force far greater than Harris's desire. Harris Bigg was not the man she loved. And she could not, as Cassandra had wisely declared, marry a man she did not love.

By the time the maid came in Jane had given up trying to sleep. The looking-glass showed her red-rimmed eyes. But she did not flinch from what she had to do. She waited until the household had begun to rise. Then she dressed and packed her remaining belongings for the journey. Tiptoeing downstairs, she sought out Elizabeth, who always brought her small son down to have breakfast with his grandparents, and, leaving him in their charge, walked in the loggia, reading prayers.

"Why, Jane, what is it?" she asked in astonishment. "Why are you dressed to depart? Where is Cass?"

"Elizabeth, help me," pleaded Jane. "Please would you find Harris, and bring him to the library? I must speak to him."

Elizabeth was wise enough not to pursue her questioning. She shut her book and departed, and Jane made her way dejectedly to the library, where she sat down on a studded leather chair, her bonnet in her hand. She did not want to stay in the house one more minute, but she could not leave without doing the honourable thing by Harris.

"Good morning," he said, shutting the library doors behind him. When he came near her, his expression changed. "My dear Jane, are you well?"

"I am quite well, but I cannot marry you."

He sat down heavily. "You have changed your mind?"

She tried to collect her thoughts. Hours of rehearsing her phrases were as nothing; they had vanished from her memory. She resolved to trust instinct instead. "Sir, I have made a mistake."

"Do not address me as sir." He leaned forward, his elbows on his knees, his hands clasped with such constriction that the fingers showed red. "After last night."

Jane could scarcely bear the expression of his eyes: bewildered, disbelieving, yet trusting. "I realize now that I was not being truthful, to either you or myself, when I agreed to become your wife," she said.

He did not speak. No trees rustled outside the library windows, no housemaid swept the stairs. In the eerie silence it seemed to Jane that she and Harris were the only living beings left on earth. But even if they had been, she could not marry him.

She saw him draw breath. She knew she must speak before he did. "When I accepted your proposal, which I assure you I was most honoured to receive, my thoughts were cast in an altogether wrong direction."

"Wrong?" He swallowed hard. He was trying to understand.

"I was thinking of another marriage, not ours."

She looked into his face. His expression had changed. Not unexpectedly, disbelief had turned to suspicion as he waited, as still as a statue, for her next words.

"Recently a marriage took place, far away in Ireland. The news of this marriage clouded my perception of what was right. I resolved that I would do everything in my power to secure a husband, now that I could no longer hope…"

Her voice broke. She could not go on. Before she could recover her composure Harris had left his chair and was kneeling on the carpet beside her. She found her bonnet knocked from her fingers, her hands taken up and kisses bestowed upon them. "Jane, Jane," he urged, "you must not speak of this. If this man is now married to another, turn to a new hope – of marriage to a man who holds you very dear."

She could say nothing. Tears wetted her face, and splashed onto the gloved hands which Harris still clasped. Barely in control of his own voice, he whispered, "And what of *my* hope, Jane?"

"Stop!" she blurted, pulling away her hands. "Sir, I cannot be prevailed upon to revise my decision. Make no further appeals to me; to do so will increase the unhappiness of us both."

Agitated beyond polite endurance, she retrieved her bonnet and stood up. As she did so her skirts brushed the kneeling man's face; resolutely she swept them aside. The room blurred into a maze of light and colours as she crossed to the door; she did not think to wipe the tears away.

Her hand upon the doorknob, her back turned to him, she spoke as steadily as she could. "I cannot enter married life with a man I have deceived. You are young, and will find another woman who will love you as I cannot."

She heard him take a step towards her.

"Sir, I beg you!" she implored, turning.

He was standing in the centre of the room, his face as white as his necktie, his hands hanging by his sides. But he was astute enough, and proud enough, to recognize defeat. "Very well," he said solemnly. "I release you from your engagement."

"Thank you," she whispered.

They faced one other. His eyes searched hers, but he said nothing.

"I will make my peace with God and with my conscience," she said. "If you will forgive me."

He nodded.

"I travel to Steventon with my sister within this half-hour."

He nodded again.

"We shall visit Manydown again, though perhaps not for a long time."

"I understand," he said, without expression. His eyes looked like a blind man's. Jane and Cassandra were his sisters' friends, he must expect them to come and stay at his parents' house. But, being a man, he could make sure he was from home when they did. And once Manydown was in his hands, any hospitality extended to them would be his prerogative, not his family's. He would never have to see Jane again if he did not choose to do so.

Cassandra did not ask what had happened. When their goodbyes had been said, and the carriage had rumbled between the gateposts of Manydown, she allowed her sister to collapse against her shoulder. Exhausted, and chastened by the knowledge that she had inflicted unhappiness upon a man whose only folly was to fall in love with her, Jane allowed the movement of the carriage to soothe her like an infant in a cradle.

At the end of the journey back to Bath, life would go on. And it mattered little whether Jane ever wrote another story, since her three completed novels were still hidden in their box. Sometime, when she did not feel sleepy as she did now, and when only Cassandra was in the house, ready with her praise and criticism, she would open the box. She would resurrect Elinor and Marianne, and Jane and Elizabeth and Catherine from their grave, and make them live. And in their lives, she would live hers.

"What was the name of that publisher Papa mentioned?" she asked her sister drowsily. "A Mr Murray, was it?"

"Go to sleep," murmured Cass. "And stop thinking."

"I can do the first, but not the second," said Jane, and closed her eyes.

Epilogue

_N_either Jane nor Cassandra ever married. *Elinor and Marianne* was given the new title of *Sense and Sensibility* and published in 1811, generating interest among critics and delight among the public. This was followed in 1813 by Jane's biggest success, *Pride and Prejudice*, which started life, of course, as *First Impressions*. *Northanger Abbey*, as *Catherine* was eventually titled, did not come out until after Jane's death in 1817 at the age of forty-one.

The Austens remained without a permanent home after the Reverend Austen's death in 1805, then in 1809, with Edward's help they secured a cottage at Chawton in Hampshire, not far from Steventon. Once settled there with her mother, sister and Martha Lloyd, Jane returned to writing. She revised and published her first two novels, and produced three other books, two of which, *Mansfield Park* and *Emma*, were published during her lifetime. The remaining book, *Persuasion*, joined *Northanger Abbey* in the same posthumously published volume.

And what of Cassandra? Considering herself the widow of a man she had never married might seem extreme, but this dramatic action did not detract from the support, good sense and devotion she unstintingly bestowed upon her only sister. She outlived Jane by twenty-eight years and her mother by eighteen, living alone at Chawton until her own death in 1845.

The cottage at Chawton is now a museum devoted to Jane and her works. Steventon Rectory met its own demise only six years after Jane herself, in 1823, when it was demolished to make way for a new house. Jane might well see it as fitting that although the place in which she wrote some of the world's favourite novels does not exist any more, its influence lives on in her pictures of "three of four families in a country village".

As for the other principal characters in this book, they are real. Twelve years after this story ends, Jane's niece Anna married Madam Lefroy's elder son, Ben. Still later, in 1828, Martha Lloyd became the second wife of Frank Austen. His brother Charles also married twice, and Jane's estimate of a large number of future nieces and nephews was accurate. In all, the Austen brothers produced over thirty children.

We cannot know which young gentlemen touched or did not touch Jane's life, nor what they said and did; but there is no escaping Willoughby, Bingley and Darcy, or even Mr Collins, who show themselves as confidently in fiction as Jane herself hides her life in shadow. The last service Cassandra performed for her sister was to destroy as many of her letters as she could find, in the hope of keeping private details secret, so our factual knowledge of Jane's life has been pieced together from other sources by painstaking scholars.

Jane would appreciate the irony that it is Cassandra, who, by keeping the facts from us, has given us what Jane herself so cherished – the power of imagination.

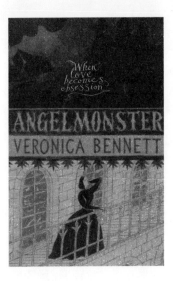

I saw no one but him, dreaming or waking. I fell in love so madly, I almost did not recognize it as love. It was madness and nothing else.

Mary and her sister Jane have always longed for a handsome young man, preferably a poet, to whisk them away from their mundane life. Then, in the spring of 1814, Percy Shelley walks into their father's shop, like an angel of deliverance. Seduced by Shelley's radical ideas – freedom from marriage and the binds of religion – the girls flee with him to Europe.

But when tragedy strikes, Mary begins to realize that her dreams have become nightmares – and her angel ... a monster.

"Those in search of a good story need look no futher." *The Guardian*

"A haunting story, beautifully written and rich in historical detail." *The Bookseller*